MR JANUARY

Calendar Boys Series

NICOLE S. GOODIN

Mr. January
Published by Nicole S. Goodin
ISBN: 978-0-9951168-1-8
Copyright 2019 by Nicole S. Goodin
All rights reserved. ©
First published January 2019

Cover design by Nicole Goodin
Images purchased from Shutterstock
Editing by Spell Bound

For all the babes born in January

CHAPTER ONE

Andy

I lift my head and frown as I hear yelling from outside the office door.

It sounds like a woman, and a pissed off one at that.

I don't know what the hell is going on out there, but in my experience, there's only one place you want to hear a woman screaming – and that's in the bedroom.

"That's gotta be your fault." Jeff shoots me an accusing look and I shrug at him.

I've had my fair share of woman dramas over the years, but being locked up in a jail cell for the past three years put a swift fucking end to my love life.

"I know that bastard's in there, and I don't care if I get sent to prison myself, I'm going to damn well get what I came here for," the woman yells.

"That's got you written all over it, Wood," he warns me.

I'm about to respond when the door to the room flies open and crashes against the wall with a loud bang.

The curvy redhead responsible for all the damn noise snarls as her gaze lands on me.

Jeff might be a total pain in the ass most of the time, but he was right – this *does* have me written *all* over it.

And thank fuck for that.

She's a sight for sore eyes.

I throw my arm over the back of my chair and lean back as I watch her, a cocky smirk on my face – I know it'll piss her off and that's the reason I do it.

Today must be my lucky day, I'd been hoping I'd get to lay eyes on that fine ass of hers soon, but I hadn't been expecting her to deliver it right to me on a plate like this.

I thought I was going to have to work a bit harder to get this little show, but maybe there's some good karma left on my side after all – then again, maybe not, given the death glare being sent my way.

"*Dylan*, what do I owe this pleasure?" I drawl.

She stalks over until she's standing right in front of me, radiating fury.

If there's one thing I've never failed to be able to do, its drive this woman wild – and it doesn't appear that anything has changed in that department.

She might be fuming mad, but fuck she is still so beautiful. She smells the same too – like strawberries and coconut. Just one moment in her personal space and I'm totally and utterly hooked on her again.

The stack of papers she's holding in her hand land down with a thud on the table, shaking the entire thing and spilling Tony's coffee all over his work.

I glance at him, but he hasn't even noticed the mess – he's too busy watching the woman causing a scene in front of everyone with his jaw dropped.

I almost feel bad for not giving my manager warning that something like this could happen – but in all honesty, he seems to be appreciating the view nearly as much as I am. I might have to give him a different type of warning.

"Cut the shit, you cocky little convict, you know *exactly* why I'm here," she hisses, drawing my eyes and my thoughts back to her.

I lazily pick up the papers she's shoved in my direction and make a show of looking them over as if I don't already know exactly what they are.

I knew what they were the moment I laid eyes on her.

They're the same papers she's sent me nearly every month for the past three years.

"Just sign the fucking papers so I can divorce your stupid ass," she says.

"Gentlemen," I announce to the room full of my staff, ignoring her demands as I do, "have you all met my wife?"

CHAPTER TWO

Dylan

"Coffee?" he asks, and I shake my head.

"Tea?"

"*No.*"

"Juice?"

"I don't want a god damn drink, Andy, just sign the papers so I can get on with my life," I snap.

He turns and glances over his shoulder at me – his signature bad-boy smirk still firmly on his face.

It's the same smirk that made me look twice all those years ago, and I hate myself for the little flip in my belly it still causes.

It pains me to admit it, but prison has been kind to him. He looks *good*.

Fuck *good*, he looks incredible.

Even better than the day we met, or the day we got married for that matter. I'd been hoping he'd got fat or bald during his time inside, but instead, he's somehow only got better looking.

"You and I both know I'm not signing those." He chuckles as though the very idea of our impending divorce is a joke to him.

We haven't seen each other for three years, and even though it would seem that he's still very capable of making my insides quiver, that doesn't change the fact that he's not my husband anymore.

The man that left me three years ago isn't coming back.

"Sign them." I smack my hand down on the papers, the action far more confident than the way I feel on the inside.

He turns around slowly, and I can feel my heart rate accelerate in my chest at the very thought of him coming closer to me.

Yip, I really do hate myself.

I ready myself to step back away from him, but he doesn't come any nearer, instead turning, so he's resting his hip against the counter top.

He crosses his arms arrogantly against his chest as he continues to stare at me with those familiar brown eyes.

The muscles in his forearms tense and bulge, and I have to swallow deeply to keep from drooling.

I can see the tattoo that runs down his bicep and I know I shouldn't care, but I desperately want to see the rest of it again.

Shit.

I need a pep talk, and pronto.

This encounter is heading into dangerous territory and he hasn't even attempted to touch me yet – the well thought out plan I had in my mind is heading south, fast.

I try to picture my friend Sarah in my mind. She'd tell me that I'm a strong, independent woman who 'doesn't need no man' – complete with side-to-side finger snaps.

Only right now I don't feel all that independent or strong, in fact I feel weak, like an alcoholic looking at a glass of whiskey.

And Jesus Christ I'm *thirsty*.

"You're a smart woman, Dylan, you know I'm not signing those papers, so why did you really come here?"

He steps forward now, and it's all I can do not to turn and flee. I try to stand a little taller. The last thing I need is for him to think he's got the upper hand over me again. Even if the reality is that he does.

I watch him prowl towards me as though I'm his prey, and the frightening thing is, I *am*.

"How'd you know where to find me?"

"Jeff," I say. "Your sidekick told me you'd be here."

I probably shouldn't throw Jeff under the bus, especially since he clearly didn't rat me out, but it's too late now, my mouth has answered him before my brain even considered that I shouldn't.

"You didn't visit," he murmurs as he approaches.

I'm not sure if it's intentional or not, but there's an edge of hurt to his tone. It makes me feel guiltier than I'd like it to.

"Prison isn't really my scene."

"You didn't call."

"I had nothing to say," I reply.

He's so close to me now, and just like I feared, all I can smell is his stupid, intoxicating, manly scent.

My mind floods with memories of falling asleep and waking up to the very same smell – it's been hard enough to forget those little things when he was gone, let alone now, when he's close enough to touch.

He's still wearing his ring, and while I hate that he is, part of me is elated that he still considers himself taken – that's how fucked up my brain is.

He reaches out and runs his fingers slowly down my bare arm.

I shudder. There's nothing I can do to stop it. I don't want to be affected by him, but it's the way I'm wired. There's just something about him that connects to a hidden part of me that nobody else knows about.

No other man has ever evoked this type of reaction in me.

I've tried to move on, I really have, but no one else has come anywhere close.

"*Please* sign the papers," I plead with him in a whisper, abandoning my former tactic of appearing strong and in control.

"You know I can't do that," he says.

His voice is deep and gravelly; it's the very voice that makes me crave him.

I don't want to ask him, but the question falls from my lips without my permission. "Why not?"

"You're *my wife*. Three years in a jail cell doesn't change that," he growls.

He's wrong. Him leaving me for all that time *did* change things.

Everything changed the moment he decided that being a thief was more important than being my husband.

I can't let him walk all over me and weaken me with his sex appeal.

I have to stay strong.

I can almost feel my spine straighten as my resolve strengthens.

"It changed things for *me*," I tell him.

I brush his hand off from where it sits on my skin and round the small table, putting a solid barrier between us.

His hand lingers in thin air before dropping to his side.

He sighs.

"I want a divorce," I say.

"I don't." He almost growls the words.

"I guess we'll have to go to court then."

I make the mistake of looking at him again and I'm surprised to see his usually cocky expression is missing from his face.

He looks so handsome when he's vulnerable, and I know I need to get out of here right now before I do something really, really stupid.

A raw, real Andy is far more threatening to my self-control than an arrogant one could ever be.

I point to the papers. "I'm leaving them. I want them signed by tomorrow."

I turn on my heel and I'm almost safely out the door before I hear him speak again.

"You never even asked me if I did it or not."

I pause for a fraction of a second.

He's right – I didn't ask him. He was guilty. I didn't *need* to ask him.

I *could* ask him now, but I'm not sure I can bear to hear his confession.

It nearly broke me, just being told about what he'd done, but hearing those words from the man himself will be the final blow, one I can't handle.

I walk out the door and let it swing closed behind me.

CHAPTER THREE

Andy

I punch the table and swipe the stack of papers she left behind onto the floor with a swing of my arm.

I collapse into a chair and drop my head onto the table with a loud, defeated groan.

I was not prepared for this – not today.

I knew I'd see her soon, but I expected it to be on my terms – when I was ready for it – not hers.

I had no idea she even still thought of me. Other than the monthly delivery of a request for divorce, I haven't heard from my wife since I first got put behind bars.

She obviously knows more than she's let on – she knew I was out.

I might be a tattooed, stereotypical bad boy, now with the ex-con tag to match, but I'm not too tough to miss my woman.

She might have repeatedly tried to wash her hands of me, but I still want nothing else more than I want her.

I've wanted that woman from the first moment I laid eyes on her.

"She's still too hot for you, bro." A mocking voice interrupts my pity party.

I raise my hand and shoot Jeff the middle finger.

She *is* too hot for me – always has been. Her hair might be longer, and her curves a little less full, but she's still the same stunning woman she always was.

I hear his footsteps and the sound of the chair legs dragging against the flooring as he sits down opposite me.

"All the boys got a front row seat to that," I mutter. "That's just fucking great."

"They're still talking about it now. It's not every day the boss's wife comes in throwing shade around."

"Shit."

I haven't been able to be a hands-on boss for more than the past few days, and already I'm bringing drama into the garage. As entertaining as our staff might have thought it was – it's not a good look.

"I wouldn't sweat it, Wood, half of them think she's hot and the other half are scared shitless of her."

I chuckle humourlessly.

"So... she wants a divorce?"

"Nothing new there," I say.

"You gonna give it to her?"

My head rises so I can look at him. If looks could kill, the bastard would be dead. He might be my oldest buddy, but if he's going to say shit like that, I'll have to knock his head in. He's already talked to her behind my back and then neglected to mention it to me. As far as I'm concerned, he's had his first strike.

"I'll take that as a no," he says quickly.

"You can take it as a *fuck no*."

He nods and leans back in his chair. "I was just asking. Don't go getting your knickers in a knot, precious."

I glare at him.

"You could have given me a heads up."

"You're right. I could have." He shrugs.

I narrow my eyes at him. "You on her side now?"

"Don't be a child. There are no sides... She's hurting, man."

"*She's* hurting? I'm the one who spent years behind bars *and* lost my fucking wife in the process. This hasn't exactly been a great time for me either, for fuck's sake."

"That's on you, Wood. It's like I always told you... you play with fire long enough, you're gonna get burnt – but you've always been the type of dumbass that has to learn things the hard way."

"Yeah, yeah, I fucking know. And that's all well and good now – but what's done is done. She just wants to be rid of me, a quick, easy end."

"Don't go thinking it wasn't tough on her, man, it was hard enough for me to watch. I can't even imagine how much pain she was in."

"She didn't watch though, did she? She just walked away," I snap.

None of this is his fault, and I know I shouldn't be acting like such a prick, but I can't seem to stop myself.

"If you believe that then you're an even bigger idiot than I am," he states calmly. "She might not have come in to see you like I did, but she didn't just stop thinking about you. I'd put money on that."

My wife might have disowned me when I got put away, but Jeff was always there. Every single week. He's a know it all prick, but he's the best mate a guy could ask for – not that I'd tell him that. He's always had my back. No questions asked.

"I just want her back."

He stands up and wanders over to the coffee machine. "Your ugly ass managed to seal the deal with her once. Figure out how to do it again."

"Just like that?"

"Just like that."

"She wanted me to kiss her today."

He snorts a laugh. "Whatever helps you sleep at night."

Her brain might be warning her to steer well clear of me, but her body undoubtedly is still mine, that much I know for sure. She still shakes under my touch.

If there's one thing I know about Dylan, it's that she's stubborn as hell, and if I'm going to get her back, I'm going to have to fight hard – and *dirty*.

My woman always liked it dirty anyway.

"I'm afraid to ask what's going through that fucked up mind of yours," Jeff drawls.

"You don't want to know." I grin wickedly.

"You know what I *do* want?"

I tilt my head and raise my brows at him.

"To shut down this little therapy session and go back to running a fucking business. You think you can manage that, sugar plum?"

CHAPTER FOUR

Dylan

"You can do this."

"I can do this," I repeat.

"He has *no* control over you."

I almost laugh. He has *all* the control over me, as much as I hate to admit it.

I glance at Sarah sheepishly.

"Say it," she demands in her usual no bullshit manner.

I take a deep breath and lie through my teeth. "He has no control over me."

"You're a terrible liar." She groans.

I grimace.

"He's a thief and an asshole, D, you're better off without him."

Logically I know she's right, but those two years I had with him were the most passionate, love filled, *infuriating* years of my life. All my best days have been with him.

He's always brought out the best and the very worst in me at the same time.

He's got a unique ability to drive me crazy on both ends of the spectrum – I never could quite decide if I loved him more than I hated him.

"You *are* better off without him, right?" She waves her hand in front of my face, snapping me from my trance.

"Um, I think so?" I wince.

"Oh *Jesus.*"

"I know," I mutter in agreement.

She narrows her eyes at me. "He looked good, didn't he?"

It's my turn to groan now. I don't even bother lying. "Even better than before. He looks like he's been at a fitness retreat this entire time."

"Seriously? I didn't think that man could get any hotter."

I smack her arm and grin at her. "Well he did. Oh god, what am I going to do?"

She sits her hands on her hips and gives me the 'this is what's going to happen' look.

"You're going to march that sweet ass of yours back into whatever dirty, little hovel he's hanging out in and get him to sign those papers, you got it?"

"But that's the thing... he's not slinking around in some dodgy dump. I barged into some type of business meeting, Sare."

"*What*? Who the hell wants to do business with a guy fresh out of the slammer?"

"Some guy called Tony?" I shrug. "A few other guys I didn't know... and..." I pause for dramatic effect. "*Jeff.*"

I wait for her reaction. The only thing I think my best friend hates more than my soon-to-be ex-husband is his side kick.

"Well then... *no* surprises there," she mutters as she shoots daggers at me. "Those two haven't got a set of morals between them."

I bite my lip to keep from laughing.

This might possibly be the least funny situation I've ever found myself in, with a divorce looming at only twenty-six years old, but I still can't help but have a little giggle at Sarah's pissed-off expression.

Her and Jeff were a thing for all of five minutes, but instead of making it down the aisle like Andy and I, they went up in flames and came down firing – mainly at one another.

As much as I'd like to jump down the rabbit hole that is Sarah and Jeff, right now I've got bigger fish to fry.

This isn't one of those problems I can hide from forever.

I need him to sign – the sooner the better.

"He's been out five days, Dylan, how the hell is he in a business meeting already?"

It's the question I've been asking myself ever since I walked out of that building, and I still don't have an answer.

I shrug.

"You're a journalist." She smirks. "Maybe it's time you found out."

***

"Stu, I need a favour," I announce as I bustle myself into his office.

"You *always* need something," he says.

"I know, I know... and I'm going to need it faster than you managed last time."

He raises his brows at me over the top of the magazine he's flicking through.

"*Please?*" I add in a sickly sweet voice.

He looks at me as though he's waiting for me to beg further.

"Oh c'mon," I moan, "it's not like you've got anything better to do by the looks of things."

"You're lucky you've got that red hair, you know? It explains why you've got such a short fuse."

"Oh, ha ha."

He tosses the magazine onto his desk and gives me his full attention.

"Alright, what's his name and date of birth?" he asks.

I frown at him. "How'd you know it was about a guy?"

"Oh sweetie, a woman's face looks that pissed off," he points at me, "it's *always* about a man."

I roll my eyes but don't bother denying it. You can't argue with the truth.

"Andrew Woodman," I tell him.

I know he won't recognise the name right away – I use my maiden name at my job and I've worked hard to ensure I'm not linked to a criminal in any way.

"Oooh..." He winks at me. "You know I like my men with a good bit of wood."

"How do you like your women then?" I tease.

"With red hair and a booty," he says as he scrawls Andy's name down on a pad of paper along with the date of birth I know off by heart. "So, who is this guy and what's he done to my favourite journo?"

"I want to know everything you can find out about what he's been up to in the past three years. In particular, any businesses he may have created or invested in."

He raps his fingers on the edge of his desk. "I'll have it to you within the hour."

"Thanks, Stu." I ignore his questions and turn on my heel to leave him to it.

"So, who is he?"

I sigh in defeat. I could say nothing, but there's a reason I came to Stu, he's the best – it's only going to take him a matter of minutes to figure it all out anyway.

"He's my husband," I growl as I stalk out of his office. "And I want his ass handed to me on a silver platter."

"Oooooh, *girl*." I hear Stu laugh as I disappear down the hallway.

CHAPTER FIVE

Andy

I'm on my back, tucked half under the body of the car I'm working on when I hear the familiar sound of heels clicking against concrete.

It's like déjà vu.

I heard that very sound before I first laid eyes on her. Back when I wasn't much over twenty-two years old. She walked that sweet body of hers into the garage I was working in, and as they say, the rest is history.

"This is almost *too* tempting," she says. "You know, I bet I could release this jack and make it look like an accident that you were crushed to death."

I push with my feet so the creeper rolls me out from underneath the engine.

I'm pretty confident she's joking, but you just can't be too careful when it comes to disgruntled wives as far as I'm concerned.

"Two visits in as many days. You making up for lost time?" I say as I jump agilely to my feet.

Her eyes rake over my face and down to my grease-smeared bare chest.

"I see you still haven't learnt how to wear clothes," she says, her tone full of unimpressed sass, but her eyes alight with desire.

I can't help the sly smirk that spreads over my lips.

"Or wash yourself for that matter." She rolls her eyes dramatically, but I don't miss the slight blush staining her cheeks as she's caught checking out my half-naked body.

Looks like I'm not the only one who's reminiscing about the old days after all.

"No broken-down car this time, princess?" I wink at her.

She narrows her eyes at me but doesn't answer.

That's what brought her to me all those years ago – her piece-of-shit broken-down hatchback. I worked for hours on that hunk of junk – all to buy myself more time with its owner.

"What? No trip down memory lane?"

"Memory lane is *closed*," she snaps.

She strolls past the bonnet of the car I'm working on and runs the tip of one of her fingers over the glossy paint.

I can't even explain why the simple, non-sexual gesture makes my dick jump in my jeans, but it does.

"Although... I did happen to take a small stroll into the past three years... I see you've been a busy boy."

"You keep tabs on people for a living, Dylan, do you expect me to believe that you didn't do the same for me?" I smirk at her.

"You can believe whatever you want, Andy," she answers, her tone tired. "But I'm telling you, I haven't asked about you once."

My ego takes a hit as I look at her and realise she's telling the truth.

She hasn't asked about me.

The old Dylan would have known every little detail about me the minute it became available.

Apparently, the new Dylan isn't as bothered with me as the old one was.

The fact that she didn't know anything prior to showing up here yesterday only reinforces my hunch that she really has been trying to erase me from her life for good this time.

It causes a physical ache in my chest to think about having any kind of life without her – but it's pretty fucking clear that she doesn't feel the same way anymore.

In fact, the only thing it seems she knows about me and my time spent behind bars, prior to right now, is that I finally got out, and considering she *hasn't* been keeping an eye on me, I don't even know how she found that out.

My parole office didn't tell her – I know that much, and she changed her cell-phone number the minute I got locked up, so even if I'd wanted to call her and tell her myself, I couldn't.

I would blame Jeff for it, but I've got his word that he didn't tell her anything other than where she could find me. She was already armed with the information of my release.

"How'd you know I was out?"

She spins around to face me. Her expression tells me she's surprised at my choice of question.

The corner of her lip twitches as though she's debating whether or not to give up her source. "Bruno," she exhales on a laugh.

"Bruno, as in the warden?"

She winks at me. "He owed me a favour."

I wasn't expecting her to say that. I know full well that Dylan has contacts all over the city, but I didn't think even she had a reach quite that long.

I grin at her. "Are you sure you haven't been spying on me the whole time?"

"Don't flatter yourself," she says as she sways her hips over to look at the '69 Corvette parked in the corner.

"We had a deal – I only wanted to know if you got out. He told me when you went to court, and he gave me your release date. *Nothing else*." She circles the car slowly and inclines her head in the direction of it. "Nice ride."

I don't tell her that it's mine. There's a lot of heavy objects around and her temper seems to be just as fiery now as it ever was.

I might be willing to do just about anything for this woman, but if I can avoid having to repaint my baby, I will.

"So... this is a mechanics garage," she says, "and you own it."

"You didn't see that yesterday during your little hissy fit?" I raise my brow at her in question. "There's a big sign out front saying, "Woodman and Stone.""

I snag a rag off my tool station and wipe some of the grease off my hands with it.

She doesn't reply as she strolls back towards me looking every inch the sexy bombshell.

She's wearing a tight, white dress that shows off *every* curve on her body – the very same body I craved each and every night since I got put away.

"I was a little preoccupied with my rage."

"I noticed. You scared the shit out of my receptionist."

She glances in the direction of the front desk, which is visible through the window-lined wall.

"I guess I shouldn't be surprised that you've got some pretty little thing involved in whatever this is." She gestures around the garage.

"Bree," I prompt. "And if I didn't know better, I'd think you were jealous."

She laughs. "Dreams are free, Andy."

I haven't heard the sound of her laugh in three years, and I'm momentarily shocked still by something that was once so familiar to me.

It hits me hard then, just how much I've missed her.

I'd do anything to be able to touch her right now, but I know that she'd probably whack me with a wrench if I tried.

"Did you do what I asked?" She looks at me with a hopeful expression that slices deep into my heart.

I shake my head, and she closes her eyes momentarily in disappointment.

I hate myself for it coming to this between us, and I know damn well that if I'm going to get my wife back I'm going to have to be smart about it.

A woman like Dylan can't be negotiated with right off the bat – she's too stubborn and too proud for that... she has to be tempted first.

I make a show of rubbing at the grease on my abdomen with the rag in my hand. Her eyes trace down my front once again and I chuckle.

I can't blame her for taking notice, avoiding the crappy prison food and having nearly unlimited hours to work out has been kind to me. I'm in the best shape of my life.

I've had nothing but time lately and I haven't wasted a minute of it.

She huffs out a breath when she realises she's been caught staring yet again and storms off towards the other side of the garage. She pulls out a chair and inspects it for cleanliness before sitting down on it and crossing her arms across her chest.

"Not that I'm complaining about the view, but why exactly are you here, Dylan?" I ask as I pick up my drill.

"Cut the crap, Andy. You know why."

I shake my head in amusement. "Well you better make yourself comfortable, princess, because if you're waiting on my signature, it's gonna be a fucking long wait."

"I've got nowhere to be," she replies, her tone cocky.

I shrug and turn back to the car.

I don't know what game she's attempting to play – she might have been able to out wait me once upon a time – but she seems to have forgotten that I've had thirty-six months to practise patience.

"Suit yourself." I shrug as I go back to my work.

***

Credit where credit's due, she's lasted a fuckin' long time in that chair – a lot longer than I thought she would. She's only got up twice – both times to pee and she's barely eaten. Bree, who I genuinely think is scared of my wife, brought her a coffee and a sandwich; that was hours ago – all the staff have long since gone home.

Other than that, she's just sat there, staring at me as I work, as though I'm the devil himself reincarnated. The only time she stopped huffing and puffing for longer than ten minutes was when Jeff arrived.

The bastard even got a hug and a smile.

"How long you think she's gonna sit there for?" he whispers to me in a hushed tone.

"Pass me that screwdriver." I point to the tool behind him and he hands it to me. I tighten up the screw before glancing up at him. "I dunno, man, probably all night if she thinks it's getting to me."

"*Is it* getting to you?" He smirks at me.

"Not nearly as much as you are," I quip.

"What are you gonna do about her?"

I shrug. "Let her sit I guess."

"It's getting cold, she hasn't even got a jacket."

We both glance over at my stubborn-ass wife. She's still perched in her chair, her phone in her hand, nothing but her tiny dress and heels on.

"Not my problem. No one's keeping her here."

I thought the same thing about an hour ago, but there's no way in hell I was going to be the one to give in by offering her something warm.

"I'm gonna go find her something."

"For the love of god, don't go making her more comfortable," I hiss at him.

He ignores me and heads off in search of something to keep my wife warm and comfortable as she torments me.

"*Asshole*," I mumble.

My so-called best mate is enjoying this a little too much if you ask me. I know he cares a lot about Dylan, but right now, his nurturing bullshit isn't doing me any favours.

He comes back with a blanket which he drapes across her shoulders.

She smiles up at him like he's her favourite person in the world and I snap.

"Christ," I mutter to myself. "That's fucking *it*."

I stalk across the room towards Dylan and she shoots me a smug look from within her cosy cocoon of victory.

Jeff's lucky he's disappeared; the dude's got rocks in his head and I'm about ready to have a go at shaking them out of there.

"You really want me to sign those fucking things?" I bark the question at her.

Her eyes widen, and she blinks three times without saying anything.

I've caught her off guard and that's exactly what I need.

"Well?" I toss the engine part I'm holding on to the bench behind her and she jumps at the loud bang.

"*Yes*. I want you to sign."

"Fine, I'll sign your papers."

She visibly sags in what I assume is relief.

It cuts me deeper than I'd care to admit.

"But I've got one condition," I tell her.

"Okay..." She gets to her feet in front of me and straightens out her dress. "What is it?"

"I want one week, Dylan. I want you to give me *one* week."

"One week for what?" she asks as her eyes dart between my face and a spot off in the distance. She's nervous – I can hear the uncertainty in her voice.

"To be *my wife*," I growl possessively. "I want seven days to show you what a terrible fucking idea this divorce is. I just need a week to make you fall in love with me again."

Her jaw drops open. She looks down at her hands and then back up at me in shock.

"I'm sorry, *what*?" She shakes her head quickly like she's trying to clear it. "You think I'm going to fall in love with you in a week?"

I reach for her, but she steps away so my hand falls short.

"It only took you twenty-four hours the first time, Dylan, but I'm trying not to be cocky about it."

She laughs humourlessly. "Oh, you're trying *not* to be cocky about it?"

I like the fact that she doesn't deny what we had before. She can deny that it's not still there all she likes, but I can still feel it between us.

"We've got unfinished business. I know it, you know it, fuck... the whole world can see this isn't over between us." I rasp the words.

"Then the whole world is *blind*."

"You owe me a week, princess."

"I owe you *nothing*," she sneers.

"You left me to rot in a jail cell for three years. I think the least you can do is give me a chance." I know it's a low blow, but it's all I've got.

"You *abandoned* me for three years. I think the least you can do is sign a sheet of paper," she fires back.

I take a slow, deliberate step forward until I'm so close to her I can almost feel the bare skin on her arms against mine.

I know I have to do something, *anything*, right now to pull her in before she gets her back up and runs.

"Dylan," I whisper as I reach for her cheek and cup it in my palm.

She leans into the contact and sighs.

The simple fact that she hasn't instantly rejected my advance sends a bolt of hope shooting through me.

"We're good together, Dylan. You remember how good we are, I *know* you do."

"That was a long time ago."

"Nothing's changed," I whisper.

"We've been married for five years, more of those years have been spent apart than together." She opens her big green eyes and looks up at me. "*Everything* has changed, Andy."

"This hasn't," I growl as I grab hold of her and drag her mouth up to meet mine.

I kiss her with every ounce of pent up emotion I've got stored inside me.

I kiss her like a man who's never tasted anything so sweet.

Her hands slide up around my neck and her fingers wind into my hair as she kisses me back with so much passion I can barely think.

"Dylan," I breathe as I pull back for air.

She freezes at the sound of her name, as though it's just hit her – exactly what she's done.

Her hands slip from my neck, down to my shoulders and across my chest, so her palms are pressing against my pecs.

She shoves me – not hard enough to move me, but firm enough to let me know she wants out.

"I can't do this, Andrew," she chokes out.

I'm not even Andy anymore, I'm Andrew, and that's how I know I fucked up big time.

She pushes past me and rushes out the door.

"Dylan!" I call after her, but she's already gone and she's not coming back.

I feel dizzy, like I can't stand straight anymore. I stumble to the edge of the bench to support myself and hang my head down as I suck in some deep breaths.

My whole god damn life just walked away from me. *Again.*

I rub my hand over my face in frustration.

That was the best thing to happen to me in a long time, and I fucked it up – like I always do.

"Well, that looks like it went well."

I snap my head up and see Jeff resting his shoulder against the doorframe my wife just disappeared out of.

"You got nothing better to do than spy on me?"

"Nah, not really," he drawls.

I pick a spare part up off the bench and hurl it across the room at the opposite wall where it smashes against the tin with a loud crash.

"Feel better?"

"No."

"She'll be back."

"Will she?" I snap. "I'm just making things worse at every fucking turn."

"So you had a crack at it – you shit the bed – it happens. Dust yourself off and try again, man."

I chuckle humourlessly. I can always count on Jeff to give it to me straight.

"You reckon?"

He shrugs. "What other options have you got? Unless you want to sign those papers after all?"

"Over my dead body," I growl.

"Well then, either lie down and die, or stop being a little bitch and get the fuck on with it."

CHAPTER SIX

Dylan

"Oh my God, Sare. Oh. My. Fucking. God."

She stares hard at me, trying to figure it out, before pointing an accusing finger in my direction.

"You *kissed* him, didn't you?"

"*No*," I answer quickly.

She lets out a breath in relief.

"*He* kissed *me*."

She groans. "Jesus Christ, Dylan, I gave you one instruction, *one*."

"I know." I grimace.

"You cannot let a man that good looking get his hands on you, for crying out loud. Have you learned nothing? Do I even want to know what happened next?"

"I ran away."

Her head snaps up in surprise. "Okay... well... *good*. At least you didn't take your clothes off... it could have been a lot worse."

She's right about that. I could picture him lifting me onto the hood of one of those cars and stripping the dress from my body.

I barely made it out of there without that very thing happening.

"He told me he'd sign." I almost whisper the words.

"Well crack the champagne." She whoops. "Why didn't you open with that little snippet of goodness?"

"Because it's not that simple." I let my head fall into my hands. "He said he'll sign, but only on one condition."

"If it's goodbye sex I'm probably going to say go for it. It's about the only thing the man's ever been able to get right." She smirks.

"What are you? My pimp?" I lift my head to look at her.

"If the money's right, baby." She winks at me.

I laugh and roll my eyes at her – I can always count on Sarah to make me laugh when the shit is hitting the fan.

"He wants to play house, Sare. He thinks he can make me fall in love with him again."

She whistles low and long.

"Right? What the hell am I meant to do with that? I can't spend a whole week with him," I whine.

"Well... that *is* quite the predicament."

I pout and wait for her to come up with some type of magical solution to my problems.

"There's one major issue I'm seeing here," she finally says.

"Just the one?" I deadpan.

"Aside from the obvious..." she says. "Does he realise that you never actually fell *out* of love with him?"

I can feel my face paling as I accept the fact that I've not hid my feelings very well at all.

"I don't know," I whisper honestly.

I've been saying for years that I hate the man, but clearly, I've not fooled my best friend in the slightest.

I think I do still love him.

I always have and maybe I always will.

He stirs things up inside me that didn't even exist before he fell into my life. But it's not enough anymore – it can't be.

"So... you play house, and then he'll sign?" Sarah prompts.

"That's what he said."

She sighs and shakes her head.

"Well then, you better buckle up, baby, because you're in for a bumpy ride."

***

"*Andy.*"

The tool he's holding falls to the ground with a loud clatter as my voice reaches his ears.

He pauses a moment before turning, like he's not really sure if he heard me at all.

He turns slowly until he's facing me. His eyes rake over my face and his whole expression softens.

This is what I've always loved about him – I don't get to see it all that often, but he's got a soft spot that's reserved entirely for me.

Sometimes he looks at me like I hung the moon and the stars.

"Dylan," he breathes. "You came back."

I shrug. "I guess I'm just a sucker for punishment."

He wipes his dirty hands down the front of his overalls and while he still looks good enough to eat, I'm grateful that this time at least, he's wearing more clothes.

"You're working on a Sunday."

"I've got nothing better to do." He shrugs.

I nibble on my bottom lip – I'm nervous – just being in the same room as him does that to me.

I can't trust myself when he's around – not when he looks so good and wants me so bad.

His gaze lingers on my lips and a smirk spreads across his face. He knows my cues well – he knows exactly the effect he's having on me.

Just like that he's back to being cocky Andy.

He's a two-sided coin. One side is sweet, sensitive and soft – the other is arrogant, egotistical and sexy.

I still can't figure out which I'd choose if I had to pick just one.

"I know I should say sorry for kissing you or some shit, but I can't apologise for something that good – and I know how you get about honesty... but I am sorry if I upset you."

"Oh yeah, you're a real open book," I reply with a roll of my eyes. I ignore his half apology entirely.

He steps towards me. "I've *never* lied to you, Dylan."

Everything about him screams sincerity in this moment, but I know I can't believe him. I'm not some young, naive little girl anymore – I have to think with my brain and not my heart where Andrew Woodman is concerned.

I jut my chin out and ignore his comment. "I'm here about your deal."

"Good... you wanna live at my place or yours?" He smirks. "Actually, it doesn't really matter, what's mine is yours, right, princess?"

I grind my teeth together and try to breathe deeply through my nose. He really is such an arrogant ass sometimes.

He's acting like he's been waiting all morning for me to show up here and accept his deal, but I know better. He was genuinely surprised to see me here. This is exactly that – an act.

I'd love nothing more than to tell him to go fuck himself, but I know I can't.

He's the most stubborn man I've ever met. He's even more stubborn than I am, and that's a big achievement. He won't give up – not without a fight – so if I want out of this marriage, I'm going to have to play him at his own game, as risky as that might be.

I'm going to have to give him his seven days.

"I've got three conditions," I say.

He waves his hand in front of himself indicating that I should continue.

"Number *one*, I'm *not* having sex with you."

He chuckles. "But what if you decide you want to?"

"Not going to happen."

"Hypothetical question," he challenges as he crosses his arms across his chest.

"*Fine.*" I grind out the word. "*Hypothetically*, if I decide I want to sleep with you – which I *won't* – then you have the green light, but do me a favour and wait to hear the actual words, mmkay, grease monkey?"

He opens his mouth to say something, some smart comment, no doubt, but I cut him off with a glare.

"Number *two*, you get seven days – not a minute more, and when those seven days are up and I still haven't fallen in love with you, you sign the papers – no questions asked, no more deals, got it?"

He nods, but I can see the pain in his eyes that he's trying to hide.

"Loud and clear."

I watch him, watching me and it takes everything I have in me not to close the gap between us and press myself against him.

I want to, so badly it almost hurts, but that wouldn't help either of us.

Passion and lust isn't going to cut it anymore. The entire foundation of our relationship has been swept away with the tide and it's never coming back.

Sex isn't going to fix that, no matter how tempting it is.

"Number three," I say. "No more lies."

"I haven't—"

"Just, *don't*..." I interrupt his plea.

He shakes his head in frustration but holds out his hand in my direction. "Deal."

I shake off the feeling that I'm literally making a deal with the devil and take his hand in mine.

CHAPTER SEVEN

Andy

"Where's the bedroom?"

She raises an eyebrow at me. "And why would *you* need to know that?"

I drop my bag to the ground with a thud. "People generally sleep in beds, princess."

She throws her head back and laughs. "Oh, this is gold, you're *unbelievable*," she mutters to herself.

I watch her with amusement – she's so fucking beautiful when she smiles.

"Nah uh, jail bird, this is your zone right here." She points to the couch in the living room.

A sly smirk crosses my face.

There's no way in hell I'm sleeping on the couch – I'm not going to get my wife back from all the way out here.

"Sorry to burst your sassy little bubble there, red, but sleeping on the couch wasn't one of your conditions."

She hates the nickname 'red', and my use of it is no slip of the tongue.

I like her when she's mad – I always have. Mad or turned on is the only way I seem to be able to get her to drop the wall she's put up between us these days.

"You ever call me that again and you'll be sleeping in the gutter out front," she warns.

I hold up my hands in surrender, but I can't seem to wipe the stupid grin off my face – this woman really does bring out the worst in me.

"Fine, but I'm not sleeping on that fucking couch."

"Well please yourself, but you're sure as shit not sleeping in my bed."

She turns and struts from the room and disappears from sight.

"Oh but, princess?" I call after her. "It's *our* bed. Remember?"

I hear her slam a door and I chuckle.

This might just be fun after all.

***

I rub the towel through my wet hair as I step out of the bathroom and stroll across the hallway to Dylan's bedroom.

Tonight, I start phase one of my plan to win my wife back.

I'm going to cook.

This apartment that I guess I technically own half of has a really fancy-ass kitchen in it, and I plan on showing my woman exactly what I can do.

I push the bedroom door open with my elbow and pick up my bag from the spot on the floor where I dumped it.

I empty the contents out across the bed and flick through the mess looking for something clean to put on.

"Jesus Christ, did you develop an allergy to clothing while you were locked up?"

I startle and look around for her, in all my naked glory.

I find her sitting in the chair by the window, her iPad in her lap.

She's got her hands covering her eyes, but I can see her peeking out from between her fingers.

She's not fooling me – she likes looking as much as I like showing.

I make a show of drying off the last of the water in my hair and then dropping the towel to the ground rather than using it to cover myself up.

"I know what you're trying to do," she grumbles.

"And what's that?" I chuckle as I grab a pair of boxer briefs.

"You're trying to lure me back in with your penis powers."

"My fucking *what*?"

"You're trying to have me *get back on the horse* – or more to the point, get back on *your* horse."

"I didn't even know you were in here, princess, but I'm going to take that horse comment as a compliment."

She mumbles something to herself that I don't catch.

"Are you decent yet or what?" she demands after a few beats.

"As decent as the day you married me."

She removes her hands from her face and throws her head back in frustration as she takes in my still nearly naked form.

"For the love of god, Andy, you can't walk around here like that."

"I'm having a lazy Sunday at home with my beautiful wife, I can wear whatever the fuck I like."

I had intended to at least throw on some pants, but her obvious annoyance at my lack thereof has only made me more determined to stay exactly how I am.

"I'm *not* your wife," she replies in an exhausted tone.

"Law says otherwise." I wink at her as I head for the door.

"And this *isn't* your home!" she yells after me.

"Not yet, princess, but give it a week," I holler back.

***

I chuckle as she wanders barefoot into the kitchen, following her nose.

Dylan's never been one of those girls who's afraid of a good plate of food and I love that about her.

She eyes me suspiciously up and down as she approaches.

I've added a cooking apron to my attire, so she should be happy about that at the very least.

She leans over the cook top and peers into the pots and pans I have simmering away.

"It smells good in here," she finally offers.

"You sound surprised."

She leans her hip against the countertop. She's changed into a pair of tiny pyjama shorts and a tight-fit t-shirt.

She looks like fucking sex on legs.

"Considering you can't cook, I *am* surprised."

"You said it yourself, princess, things have changed."

I go back to stirring the sauce as I wait for her to crack and ask me what I mean by that.

I'm relying on Dylan's naturally inquisitive nature to get me through this week – she's more curious than she'd ever care to admit – and I'm hoping like hell that curiosity is going to extend to me.

I need her to want to know about me again.

"What is it?"

"Lamb rack," I answer with a grin.

"Oh *shit*," she whispers.

It's no coincidence that I'm cooking her favourite meal.

My wife has always been a total sucker for a piece of meat – and not just the one between my legs.

"Roast potatoes?" She nibbles on her bottom lip as she looks up at me.

I crouch down and pull the oven open wide enough so she can see that I did indeed remember the potatoes.

"You're really going all out."

I stand up so I'm directly in front of her. "I want you back, Dylan. I know that's not going to happen if I don't make an effort."

"*Andy*..." she warns.

"Just sit, okay? I'll get you a wine."

"Fine." She sighs in defeat. "Loosen me up with alcohol; it's not like it would be the first time."

She sits down on one of the stools and I pour her a large glass of red.

I can feel her eyes on me as I work and it's doing crazy shit to my pulse. I'm jumpy and on edge and for a guy like me – a guy who's normally calm and in control – it's driving me crazy.

"Okay, I'll bite," she finally says. "Where'd you learn to cook?"

"The slammer," I say as I turn to face her.

A wave of something painful crosses her face before she gets her shit together and looks at me somewhat normally again.

"They let you cook in there?" she questions.

"Gotta fill the days somehow – I worked in the kitchen."

"Huh... I would have thought they'd have a workshop or something."

"They did. I chose the kitchen."

She takes a sip of her drink and watches me carefully.

"*Why*?"

"You always said you wanted a man that could cook."

She almost chokes on her mouthful.

"You learnt to cook, for *me*?"

"You might have tried to forget about me, princess, but everything I did in there was for you – for *us*."

"Well then..." She glances around awkwardly before taking another big mouthful of her drink.

"Tell me about the garage," I hear her say after a few minutes of silence.

"What do you want to know?"

I leave the cooking and sit down opposite her. I open one of the beers I bought earlier today.

"What do you wanna know?"

"You own a business," she states.

I take a pull of the golden liquid. "Technically *we* own a business."

Her eyes widen in surprise. "You put *my* name on it too?"

I chuckle. "What? Your little detective didn't tell you that part?"

She shakes her head slowly. "He didn't."

"*He*?" I question. "What happened to Gina?"

Gina was her side kick when I got put away – they worked together, and Gina was the woman Dylan used to do all her digging around.

"I changed jobs two and a half years ago."

"What? *Why*?"

I might have been missing in action for three years, and there's bound to be things I don't know about, but this news truly surprises me. Dylan loved her job at the magazine, I never would have guessed that she'd leave.

Her eyes glass over and she shakes her head. "It was just time for a change."

"Princess, what's wrong?"

She shakes her head again, this time with more emphasis. "Nothing. I'm fine."

She's *not* fine. I've fucked up a lot in my life, but I'm still not stupid enough to think that there's not something upsetting her right now.

"Dyl—"

"Leave it," she snaps. "I want to hear about the garage."

I watch her for a long moment and consider pressing the issue further, but I know it'll be a waste of her time – I can't force Dylan to talk to me if she doesn't want to. The woman is like a vault.

"Jeff did most of the hard work – he owns half the place," I explain to her. "But I'm sure you've figured that out already."

"How long has it been running?"

"About a year. I've got your share of the profit put aside. I'm fucking shocked with how well it's doing."

"I'm glad it's successful, but I don't want your money, Andy."

"It's not just *my* money."

She looks at me and I can see just how tired she is. She looks exhausted, whether it's down to me or something else, I don't know.

"Have you been sleeping okay, princess?"

She ignores my question and takes another large gulp of wine.

"How'd you manage to set up a business from behind bars?"

We're back to talking about me again.

"Jeff picked my brain and ran all the decisions by me... it wasn't easy, but we got there in the end... I invested my half of the money."

I can still remember the day Jeff told me about the unexpected deposit into my bank account.

It felt like the final nail in the coffin.

She'd sold our house. The house we'd restored from the ground up together.

The house we planned to raise our family in.

The house we swore we'd never leave.

She looks at me sheepishly before diverting her gaze to something on the bench in front of her.

"You sold the house," I whisper, not even attempting to hide the hurt in my voice.

We might have argued non-stop the entire time we worked on that place, but that was just one of the things I liked most about it.

"I had to."

I still don't know why she left her job, and having my income disappear can't have been easy for her – for all I know, she got into major debt.

"Did you need the money?"

I don't know the exact figure she got for our home, but assuming the money she gave me was half, then it was a hell of a lot.

She stares right at me now, her green eyes looking defeated. "Times were tough for a bit there, but it wasn't only about the money... I just couldn't be *there* without *you*."

I'm a hard guy. I don't cry about shit, but hearing those words come out of her mouth almost breaks me.

"You left me, Andy. I didn't know what to do, I didn't know where to turn."

"You should have turned to *me*."

I reach for her hand, but she snatches it back.

"I couldn't."

"You should have talked to me."

"I couldn't!" she yells this time. "You were locked up. You weren't there for me."

"You weren't there for me either," I reply, my own voice rising.

"Don't you put that on me, Andy. You made your choices."

"You didn't even hear me out."

I sound defeated. My voice has lost all volume – it's barely a whisper.

She's made up her mind about me – I can see that now, and I'm not sure there's anything I'm going to be able to do to change it.

"You want to know why I didn't stick around and hear your side of the story, *Andy*? Do you really want to know?"

I'm not sure if I do or not, but my mouth replies without my permission. "Yes."

"I'll tell you why... I *couldn't* sit there and ask you if you did it, because if you said yes, then I'd be in love with a criminal, and what kind of person would that make me? I *had* to cut you off. I just had to."

Her response might not make sense to a lot of people, but it makes sense to me.

It's self-preservation at its finest.

If she gave me a chance to talk, she wouldn't have been able to walk away – no matter if I was guilty or innocent.

Her only option for a clean break was to walk away entirely and believe that I was guilty.

I can understand why she didn't question the court ruling – it's not as though I haven't made bad calls in the past, and I was literally caught red handed.

It was all tied up in a neat little bow.

The thing that hurts the most is that I never could have walked away from her the way she did me – no matter what she'd done – yet she managed it.

I stand up from my seat and go back to the cook top.

That's enough of the deep and heavy for one evening – my head can't take any more of it. Neither can my heart if I'm being honest.

"So, Jeff got things up and running from out here and I did whatever I could from the inside. I trusted him with the money side of things and with hiring the staff."

"*Andy...*" she whispers.

I don't turn.

"And now that I'm out I'll be in the garage working five days a week, just like Jeff and Tony and the other guys."

"Well I'm happy for you," she replies softly.

"Thanks, princess," I mutter.

"Andy?"

I turn around to face her.

She looks like she wants to say something but stops herself. "Can you let me know when dinner's ready?"

I nod.

She jumps off her stool and hurries from the room.

CHAPTER EIGHT

Dylan

"I can feel the guilt creeping in, Sare, I feel *horrible*."

"Don't you dare. You've got nothing to feel bad about," she reassures me down the phone.

"But what if I do? What if I've been wrong this whole time?"

"We've been over this one hundred times, D, they caught him riding the stolen bike for crying out loud. They linked him to the entire operation. He did it. You're just being swayed by his husky voice and bangin' body."

She's right – I'm not thinking with my head, yet again.

"It is *so* bangin'." I sigh.

"He's still refusing to wear clothes I take it?"

"Mmm hmm. *And* he cooked."

"Oh *Jesus* take the wheel," she says.

"Right?"

"You're screwed."

"I'm *totally* screwed."

I hear a knock at the door to my apartment.

"Someone's here," I tell Sarah.

"As tempting as it was to come and see the show myself, it's not me."

I hear the sound of the latch on the door being opened.

"Hey, ah... is Dylan here?" a male voice asks.

"Oh shit," I hiss down the phone.

"What?"

"It's Justin."

Sarah erupts into laughter. "Oh hell, things are about to get interesting."

"I gotta go," I say as I hang up the phone.

This is *not* great timing for him to be popping in for one of his visits.

My sexy-as-hell, flirty neighbour is at the door, which has just been answered by my presumably half-naked soon-to-be ex-husband.

Fuck my life.

I rush out of my bedroom and into the hallway as I hear Andy inviting him in.

"Nah that's cool, bro, I'll catch her another time," Justin tells him.

I guess he's a smart man after all.

Andy hears me coming and glances at me over his shoulder.

He's still only wearing a tight pair of black boxer briefs, and even though this is an entirely inappropriate time to be admiring the view, I just can't seem to help myself.

"Ah, here she is." He looks back at Justin. "Princess, your friend is here," he tells me.

I have to bite back a retort at his use of my pet name in front of Justin. I know it'll only make him more inclined to do it again if I complain, so I say nothing.

I push my way around my annoying house guest and smile brightly at my neighbour.

"Justin, hey, how's it going?"

His eyes rake over my body and it's then that I realise Andy's not the only one who's a little under dressed.

I feel Andy stiffen next to me as he too notices Justin's wandering eyes. His arm is holding the door open above my head and it doesn't appear he's going anywhere anytime soon.

"Hey, Dylan." He nods and glances between me and Andy.

"Oh, this is Andy. Andy, Justin." I gesture.

"I live next door," Justin tells him as he extends his hand.

Andy takes it and shakes it firmly. "Cool. I'm Dylan's husband."

Justin's eyes widen and his jaw goes slack.

"I didn't realise you were married," he says as he looks back at me.

I could drop Andy in the deep end here and tell the incredibly handsome man in front of me that he's been in prison, but I actually think he might quite enjoy that. So I don't.

"We've been separated a few years," I explain.

Justin makes a show of glancing over my attire and then doing the same to Andy.

I can see his confusion. We don't appear separated in the slightest.

"Well... it was nice meeting you, Andy." He nods in my husband's direction. "Dylan, I guess I'll see you around?"

This is the first time we've ever had a conversation that hasn't resulted in him asking me out on a date, and I'm not sure if I'm relieved or disappointed.

"Good to meet you too, man. I'll catch you next time," Andy drawls as he shoves me out of the way and shuts the door before I have the chance to respond.

He stalks over to the couch and drops himself down onto it.

I giggle as I notice the scowl on his face.

"What?" he growls as he grabs the remote and crosses his feet at the ankles on my coffee table.

"You're jealous," I accuse gleefully.

"You've got a dude that may as well be a fuckin' male model living right next door, princess. You bet your sweet ass I'm jealous."

I watch in amusement as he mutters profanities to himself.

"He's been asking me out for close to a year," I inform him.

"I can't even blame the guy, you're fucking gorgeous."

I don't want to get flutters in my stomach when I hear those words, but I do.

"He actually *is* a male model, you know..." I bite back a laugh as I tell him.

He glances up from the TV and glares at me. "*Jesus*, Dylan, are you trying to make me feel worse?"

There's that soft spot I love so much – I'm a total sucker for him when he's unguarded like this.

"No," I reply with a shake of my head.

"What's the point of telling me that shit then?"

I know I shouldn't be doing this, flirting and giving him hope, but I can't seem to help myself.

"The point..." I tell him as I walk backwards out of the room with a flirty smile. "Is that I *never* said yes."

***

I'm being carried.

"I've got you," his husky voice tells me.

"Mmmmm," I moan sleepily.

"Shhh. Go back to sleep, princess," he whispers.

I feel myself being lowered down and tucked under the blankets.

"Drew?" I ask hopefully.

"It's me, baby. You fell asleep with your book."

I blink and try to get my bearings but it's pitch black in here. "What time is it?"

"It's around midnight."

"Why are you up?" I turn over and snuggle further into the blankets on my bed.

"I don't sleep much anymore," he whispers. "Get some more rest."

I yawn and close my eyes.

"Goodnight, princess," he whispers and I feel his lips press against my forehead as I drift back off to sleep.

CHAPTER NINE

Andy

Drew.

She called me Drew.

I haven't heard the name for longer than I'd care to admit and it shocks me to the core to hear it fall from her sweet lips now.

I'd almost forgotten about her nickname for me.

These past two days all I've gotten from her are criminal references, but not tonight. Tonight I'm *Drew* again.

I lean back against the timber headboard of her bed and sigh.

She's sleeping like a baby again.

I'm not the kinda guy who sits and watches a woman sleep while jotting down love notes – that's not me, but right now I can't take my eyes off her.

It's been way too long since I've fallen asleep and woken up next to my wife, but now that I'm here, with the opportunity to do exactly that, I seem to want to delay doing it, for just a few minutes more.

She sighs in her sleep.

"*Drew*," she breathes yet again.

I grin as I think about the first time I heard the name fall from her pouty lips.

I hear the clicking of feet against the hard concrete floor of the garage.

"Sorry, we're closed," I call out to whoever's just walked in, hours after closing time.

The clicking stops.

I roll out from under the car's engine and the sight in front of me knocks the breath clean out of me.

She's drop dead fucking gorgeous.

Long red hair, wide green eyes, curvy little body, and the sexiest dress and heels I've ever seen in my life.

She smiles as she takes a slow top-to-toe appraisal of my half-covered body.

"I'm having some car trouble... I saw your light on and I was hoping someone might be able to take a look at it?" She pulls her bottom lip between her teeth in a seductive gesture and I know damn well I'm already fucked.

She could have just asked me to help her commit a murder and I'd be asking where she wanted me to hide the body.

"I think I can help with that," I tell her as I jump to my feet.

I grab a rag and wipe the mess off my hands before sauntering over to her and extending my hand.

I half expect her to refuse my grease-covered palm, but she doesn't.

"I'm Dylan," she says as she takes my hand in hers.

"Andrew," I tell her.

"It's nice to meet you, Drew," she coos.

"It's Andrew," I correct her with a grin.

She grins back at me. "Sorry, Drew." She shrugs. "But it's stuck in my mind forever now."

I reach down and brush some of the wild red hair from her face.

She's as gorgeous now as she was then.

But she's not as trusting – that much might never be the same again.

I've done a lot of regrettable shit in my life, but losing her trust is by far the top of the list.

We can get back there, I know we can – we're still the same people – but I need time. Time I haven't got.

I need to make her remember the Drew she fell in love with and hope like hell that it's enough for her to take a chance.

***

I wake with a yawn and roll over to check the time.

7.05am.

I haven't slept more than five hours continuously in forever, but I managed it last night. I feel like I'm *finally* back home.

I can hear the light snores coming from next to me. Dylan's still asleep.

She's bound to lose her shit when she realises I'm in here, so I figure I may as well give her something to really complain about.

She's got her back to me – so I do what any good husband would and make like a big spoon.

I literally groan at the feel of her soft curves against my body.

She's so warm and familiar feeling.

She stirs in my arms and I move, just a little bit as she rolls over to face me.

"*Drew*." She smiles sleepily as her eyes land on my face.

My heart thumps against my chest.

"Good morning, princess," I whisper as I wait for this perfect moment to come to a screeching halt.

She blinks drowsily and I watch as she comes to her senses and realises exactly where she is and who's here with her.

"Andy!" she cries. "What the hell are you doing in my bed?"

I chuckle. "I told you I wasn't sleeping on the couch."

She tries to scuttle away from me, and I do my best to make it hard for her.

"Relax, princess, you fell asleep on the chair so I put you to bed, then I guess I fell asleep too."

"That's awfully convenient."

"It sure is." I wink at her.

I let her free and she rolls onto her back and stares up at the ceiling.

I throw the blankets off and take my time walking towards the door, snagging my boxers off the chair as I go.

"Oh my god, you slept *naked*?"

I turn back around so she can get a good view.

"Always have, you know that."

She huffs out a frustrated breath and throws her arm over her face to cover her eyes.

I chuckle as I resume my trip to the bathroom.

"Did you sleep naked in prison?" she calls after me.

"Depends how good looking my cell mate was," I call back with a laugh.

"I hate you."

"You love me really," I taunt her.

I take a piss and throw on my boxers before she decides she wants to inflict some real damage to something other than my hearing.

She's banging around in her room and yelling a string of curse words I can't make out.

I chuckle quietly. Same old Dylan.

I get the coffee brewed before she comes stomping out after me.

I hold up a steaming hot cup as she comes to a halt in front of me.

"Coffee?" I hold it out like a peace offering.

She narrows her eyes but takes the cup without a word.

I'm pleased to see she hasn't changed all that much since I've been gone.

Dylan was always a raging bitch before her first coffee of the day, and that's clearly still true – even if I did ask for it in this particular case.

She moans in appreciation. "You might be a total prick, but you still make coffee like a genius."

I wink at her. "You always said I was good for two things... coffee and fuc—"

"*Don't*," she cuts me off with a warning stare. "Don't even say it."

"Oh c'mon, princess." I chuckle. "Don't you wanna take my other talent for a test run? See if I've still got it?"

She plops her ass down on a bar stool and glares at me over the top of her cup. "Well when you put it like that, how could I possibly say no?"

"Sarcasm," I point out.

"Nothing gets by you." She rolls her eyes.

I take a sip of my own coffee. She's right; I'm a god damn genius.

"I'm a patient man, Dylan, I can wait."

"You'll be waiting till you're dead," she mutters under her breath.

I grin at her. I love it when she gets like this – all fire and sass.

"I'm going to work," she grumbles as she slides off her seat, still giving me the death stare.

Well shit.

Eight hours apart is not going to help me in the slightest.

I didn't think this through.

I need her with me, not at fucking work.

"Take the day off," I suggest as I follow after her.

She scoffs. "Unlikely."

"Please?" I try a different tact.

She stops in her tracks and spins around to face me, jabbing her finger into my chest as she does.

"Look, you hopped-up crook, there's no way I'm missing work for *you*. I *love* my job, and I'm far less fond of you."

I know her words should cut, and somewhere deep down they probably do, but at surface level, all I can do is smirk.

"If you want to sit around here in your underwear all day, then be my guest, but *I* am going to work."

She spins around again, her wild red hair whipping me across the face as she goes.

She's in the bedroom, with the door slammed closed behind her before I've even had a chance to blink.

The familiar scent of strawberries mixed with coconut has rendered me paralysed.

The woman might hate my guts, but fuck does she smell good doing it.

***

"Did you cook?"

"Of course I fucking cooked," I growl from underneath the hood of the BMW I'm working on. "It's my new superpower."

"And?"

"*And* what?"

I wipe the sweat off my brow with the back of my arm and glance up at him.

"Was she all about your meat or what?" He winks at me.

"Jesus Christ, Stonesie."

"*What*?" Jeff asks, feigning outrage. "I want to know if she rode the meat train all the way to gravy town."

It's official. My best mate is a halfwit.

"She enjoyed the food," I tell him firmly.

"And then she sampled your salami for seconds?" he asks hopefully.

I swear the guy is more concerned about me getting laid than I am.

"Talk about my wife and my dick in the same sentence again and see what happens," I warn him.

"Alright, alright... don't be so touchy, Wood." He chuckles as he goes about his business. "*Jesus.*"

It's silent for no more than a few minutes before he speaks again.

"So you slept on the couch, huh?"

"I was meant to."

"Oh, man, you didn't listen?"

I lean around the engine and cock a brow at him. "What do you think?"

He shakes his head in amusement.

"How'd that go down?"

"Like a cup of cold sick," I say.

"You're a braver man than me, Wood, I love that woman of yours to death, but *Christ* she scares me."

She scares me too, but for reasons I don't really want to think about, and ones I certainly don't want to share with the idiot in front of me.

I nod my head in agreement. "I'm one night down already and I'm not anywhere close to breaking down her walls."

"The woman's a god damn bricklayer now," he mumbles to himself.

I lean my hip against the sleek car and take stock of the current situation.

I may have fed her and slept in her bed last night, but that's the only thing I've changed about her life so far.

A meal and a bed mate isn't going to convince her we should stay married.

"She's just gonna go on with her life and wait me out," I think aloud.

He shrugs at me.

"What the fuck do I do?"

He shrugs again before picking up a wrench and crouching down to look under the Audi he's working on.

"I dunno, but you're not going to get your wife back by tinkering around in that engine, bro, I can tell you that for sure."

He's right. I know he's fucking right.

"I need the week off," I tell him as I'm hit with a plan.

He doesn't even bother to look back at me.

"You've already slacked off the whole first year, what's another week?" he goads me.

I resist the urge to throw the engine part I'm holding at him and instead settle for saying, "Thanks man, I appreciate it."

CHAPTER TEN

Dylan

I only have to take one step inside the door to be reminded that I'm not alone here anymore. The place just *feels* different with him around.

I hate to admit it to myself, but it feels nice. I've never liked coming home to an empty house.

I hastily remind myself that this isn't permanent – that by the end of the week Andy will be gone again.

And just as well too.

I narrow my eyes at the man himself as he swaggers out of the kitchen, all sex and sin, wearing no top. *Again.*

"Do you own any shirts?" I quip.

He grins wolfishly at me and my insides flip. "Welcome home, princess."

He strolls over to me and kisses me on the forehead, and I'm not entirely sure why I allow it, but I do.

I mentally scold myself for it, but frankly, I spent the night sleeping next to him – a *naked* him – so a kiss on the head is probably the least of my worries right now.

And besides, he looks *good*. *Really* god damn good.

I know he's doing this on purpose, but I can't help myself, I *have* to look as I follow after him.

He honestly never has looked quite this chiselled. I don't know what kind of workout he was doing on the inside, but his muscles are strong and bulging, his abdomen defined and firm...

"They're all out for dry clean," he tells me, amusement colouring his tone.

"Huh?" I say as I'm snapped from my little eye-fuck session.

"My shirts." He chuckles. "That's why I'm not wearing one."

"Convenient," I mutter as I slip around him.

I wander into the kitchen, following the smell of something delicious.

I almost whimper as I lift the lid on the pan of Thai chicken stir-fry.

If my husband wasn't a lousy ex-con, a thief and a liar I could seriously get used to this personal chef business.

"Wine's on the bench." His voice comes from behind me.

"*More* wine?" I ask as I wander over to it eagerly.

"Just showing you what life would be like, Dylan."

My eyes snap up to meet his as he says my name. I know I shouldn't feel the goose bumps over my skin because of it, but I do.

I pour myself a glass of the expensive-looking bottle of white and sit down.

He watches me for a few moments before sauntering over to the cook top and going back to his work.

"Did you have a good day?" he asks me.

"I *did*. You weren't there," I retort.

He looks over his shoulder at me and chuckles. "Ouch."

I swirl the wine in my glass and smile sweetly at him. "Did you manage to get through the day without breaking the law?"

"Barely." He laughs.

I can't help the genuine smile that spreads across my face. His laugh has always made me happy.

"Ah there it is." He points the spatula he's holding at me.

"What?"

"That smile. Fuck I've missed that smile."

It slowly slides off my face as we stare at one another. A few moments pass and all either of us does is look at the other.

I know this is headed into dangerous territory for me – *chemistry* type territory – but I can't pull my eyes away from him.

He takes a step in my direction and I visibly shudder.

He's going to come over here and put his lips on mine, and I'm going to let him.

My phone chirps, letting me know I have a new message and I blink, breaking the trance.

Jesus Christ.

I hear him sigh, in disappointment, no doubt.

I grab my phone and swipe it open, hoping that whoever it is, they can do a fucking great job of distracting me from the gorgeous man cooking in only a pair of low-slung basketball shorts in front of me.

From: Sare Bear

Is the sexy crim behaving himself?

I try to bite back my smile as I type out my reply.

To: Sare Bear
   See for yourself

I snap a picture of Andy's toned back, tattoos and all – which looks fucking incredible too now that I've had a good look at it – and attach it with the message.

He turns and raises a brow at me. "Did you just take a photo?"

I frown at him and feign innocence. "A photo? Of what?"

He just shakes his head at me, a smile playing on the corner of his lips and turns back around as my phone beeps again.

From: Sare Bear
   Well fuck me sideways and call me Martha. That is quite the sight.

I can't control myself this time; I break into a full blown laugh.

"That's it," he announces as he drops the spatula onto the bench top and stalks over to me. "What's so funny?"

"Nothing." I cackle.

"Doesn't sound like *nothing*." He grins.

He reaches for my phone on the bench at the same moment I do, but he's much faster than I am.

He snags it off and chuckles as he looks at the screen.

"Well, well, well, what do we have here?"

"*Andy*!" I attempt to snatch the phone from him, but he moves, quick as a cat, out of my reach.

"*Martha*, huh? *Wow*... Good to see Sarah is just as demented as ever."

"Give me that back!" I yell as I leap up, trying to reach his hand.

"What are you gonna do about it?" He chuckles as he holds the phone clear above his head.

The bastard is enjoying this. I'm not a short woman, but I'm certainly not as tall as him and no amount of jumping is going to get that phone down from there.

"What do you want, Andy?" I rest my hands on my hips and scowl at him.

He surprises me by saying, "I want a photo too."

"Whaa— what?"

"You've got one of me, I think it's only fair."

I attempt to bargain with him, "I'll delete it."

"It's too late. Sarah already has it. She's probably uploaded it to the spank bank by now."

A giggle slips out and before I know it I'm full blown laughing.

I peek up at him when my laughter finally dies down, and he's just standing there watching me, his brown eyes soft and warm, a satisfied smile on his perfect lips, and my phone still in his hand, which is now lowered to his chest.

I lunge for him, leaping against his body in an attempt to get back what's mine.

I expect to land with a thud. What I *don't* expect is to be hoisted up by my ass against his firm, bare chest.

I *certainly* don't expect to find my legs wrapped around his waist and my face only millimetres from his.

I know I shouldn't have my hands on his bare flesh, but I do, and my god it feels amazing.

"Nice try, princess," he murmurs, his voice strained.

He's so close I can feel his breath against my skin.

I can't speak. I haven't been this close to him in a long, long time – not willingly anyway – and my whole body is rejoicing at the prospect of getting even closer.

He leans in and runs his nose against the skin on my neck, inhaling deeply as he does.

I squirm against him. The intimacy, it's too much – I know I don't have the self-control to resist this if he pushes it further.

"*Jesus*, Dylan," he growls.

"Put me down," I whisper. "Please."

I watch him lick his lips and just when I think he's going to kiss me, he takes a step forward and slides my ass onto the kitchen bench top.

My hands are still gripping his biceps and his are still wrapped around my body, his naked chest flush against me.

"That was a risky little move." He lowers his face back to my neck and presses his lips softly to the spot below my ear.

I suck in a deep, ragged, breath.

"I want my photo," he whispers hoarsely in my ear as he steps away.

He holds a finger up to me, indicating that I should wait exactly where I am.

There's no mirror around, but I bet I look like I've just had a roll in the hay. I can feel the heat in my cheeks, and my hair feels like it's sticking out all over the show.

He pulls his phone out of his pocket and slides mine in, in its place.

"Andy, I'm a mess."

"You're fucking perfect." He chokes out the words as his eyes drag over my body.

"*Andy*."

"Stay still."

I could jump down and run, but I know he'll only hunt me down and find me, and if he touches me again the same way he just did, he's likely to get a photo of me wearing a lot less than what I am now.

So I stay.

"Smile," he prompts.

I've got a stomach full of butterflies, the last thing I feel like doing is smiling. I'm nervous as hell.

This man, who has seen every single part of my body, one million times over, is making me nervous – even fully clothed.

I bite down on my lip and glance at the door as I contemplate running again.

I hear the snap of a photo being taken and my eyes dart over to look at him.

He taps the screen of his phone and lets out a pained groan.

"What? Is it blurry?" I ask hopefully.

"Not even close."

I narrow my eyes at him.

"You look like a wet dream, Dylan, fuck... you *are* a wet dream."

I scramble off the counter, cheeks blushing the deepest shade of crimson imaginable.

"Well... ah... *thanks*... now give me it back."

I hold out my hand for my phone.

He reaches into his pocket and pulls it out, sliding it open rather than giving it up.

"Hang on."

"A deal's a deal, Andy," I remind him as he taps away for a moment.

"Best fucking deal I ever made." He smirks as he hands it back to me.

The phone in his hand chimes and I realise he's just ensured that my number is saved in his phone.

"Touché, Woodman, that was nicely done."

He leans in close and I'm so still I'm not even sure I'm breathing anymore.

He reaches for my face and runs the pad of his thumb over my bottom lip, dragging it down.

I know it shouldn't but it makes me crave his touch again.

He places one, soft, gentle kiss to the tip of my nose before turning around and muttering, "Best fucking deal..." under his breath.

CHAPTER ELEVEN

Andy

"Jesus, Dylan, why the fuck is it so cold in here?" I yell as I look for her in the bedroom.

It's fucking freezing in this place and I've got no idea what the hell is going on.

"*Dylan*!" I yell again as I half run down the hallway in my towel.

"Oh, you're out." She smirks at me from her spot on the couch.

She's wearing a thick woolly jumper and has a blanket draped over her.

"What in the name of God happened to the heat?"

She shrugs. "I thought it might be nice to cool things down."

"You *thought it might be nice*?" I retort. "What are you thinking?"

She bites down on her lip to keep from laughing. "That maybe it might be too cold to walk around naked...." She shrugs.

Oh she didn't...

The sneaky little minx.

"Oh, I get it," I say. "You can't handle looking at all of this." I gesture to my bare torso.

She shrugs nonchalantly.

"I cook you a nice dinner, buy you expensive wine... and this is the thanks I get?"

She giggles gleefully. "Well we can do this the hard way or the easy way, Andy. Which is it gonna be?"

"I know how you like things hard," I drawl.

"I like things *clothed*," she quips. "And until you figure out how to cover up all those muscles, it's not going to get any warmer in here."

"All *these* muscles?" I make a show of flexing my bicep at her, grinning as I do it.

I've turned into a total cheesy bastard right now, but I don't care, I'm happier than I've been in a long time – even with this chilly air.

"Mmm hmm." She nods, doing her best to appear unimpressed and not fooling me in the least.

"If I'm going to have to cover up from now on, I'd better give you a good show first..."

"Don't you dare, Andy," she warns me as I reach for my towel.

"What's that? You dare me? Well if you say so, baby," I taunt as I whip the towel from my body.

It probably wasn't my brightest move, it's that fucking cold in here my cock and balls have probably retreated back inside my body trying to find warmth, but I don't care.

I throw the towel at her on the couch and she laughs.

"Go and put some fucking clothes on, Andy. Jesus Christ."

I salute her and jog out of the room.

If she wants to play games, I can play too.

I've always been good at games.

***

It doesn't take her nearly as long as I thought it would to come and find me.

I'm tucked up warm in her bed, all settled in for the night.

It's like a chiller in this fucking place, and if she thinks I'm going to sleep on the couch then she better think again.

"Are *you* reading?" she asks in surprise.

I'd been expecting her first words to be 'fuck off out of my bed', so these words, snarky as they are, are a welcome surprise.

"Nah. It's got pictures," I retort as I shut the book I've got in my hands.

She shakes her head at me, but I don't miss the smile on her lips.

I'm starting to wear her down. I can sense it.

"What is it?" she asks as she pads closer and sits down on the side of the mattress near my covered legs.

"One of yours. I hope you don't mind?"

She raises a brow at me. "Seriously, of all the shit you've done the past two days, *that's* the thing you feel the need to ask permission for?"

"Touché." I chuckle.

She turns the book in my hands over so she can see what it is. "Ah, good choice," she praises.

I shrug; I don't know shit about books, but I do know a thing or two about impressing my woman it would seem.

She looks at me then, under her covers and narrows her eyes at me. "You're not sleeping in here."

"Oh c'mon. I'm not even naked this time, I promise."

"Good to know." She raises her brows at me, like she's still waiting for me to get up and move.

I reach over and pat the other side of the bed. "You may as well let it go, you know you can't move me, all these muscles are pretty heavy."

She rolls her eyes. "Seriously, Andy, get out."

"Seriously, Dylan, get in."

She tries to shove my legs as she giggles. "You can't sleep here."

"Well I can't sleep out in that fucking igloo. I need body heat, princess, it's survival one-oh-one."

"You're ridiculous."

"You're the one who turned the place into a fridge," I retort, a shit-eating grin on my face.

"You're not going to move, are you?"

"Not even a little bit."

She scowls and climbs over my legs to get to the other side of the bed, doing her best to dig her knees in wherever she can.

I groan as one lands a little closer to my balls than I would have liked. "Watch the crown jewels, princess, we might need them to make babies one day."

I don't know what I've said wrong, but the look on her face sends ice through my veins.

She's frozen to the spot and looks like she's going to burst into tears.

"Dylan?"

She scrambles the rest of the way over me and dives under the blanket, pulling it right up to her chin and rolling so her back is facing me.

"Dylan?" I say softly. "What did I say?"

"Nothing," she chokes out. "Just forget it. And don't touch me."

Fuck, I feel like an absolute bastard and I have no idea why.

The last thing I want to be doing is making her cry.

"I'm sorry," I whisper as I flick off the light. "Goodnight, princess."

She doesn't answer me, but I know she's not asleep.

I hear her sobbing quietly for a long while afterwards, and as badly as I want to hold her, I don't.

This isn't something I can even begin to know how to deal with.

***

"Go get dressed, there's something I want to show you today," I tell her as I shovel my last mouthful of cereal into my mouth.

She snorts a laugh. "Sorry there, cupcake, I've got work – out here in the real world we have this thing called *responsibility*."

I drop my bowl into the sink and grind my teeth together.

I want to go over and shake the snarky comment right out of her.

I know all about fucking responsibility.

I know what it's like to have it, and I know what it's like to have it taken from you.

I know what it's like to have the person you're responsible for out there in the world doing fuck knows what, and not be able to do a single thing about it.

I take another sip of coffee to calm myself down – I can't be losing my cool with her – it's not her fault my responsibilities were taken from me. That's all on me.

"Not the rest of this week you don't," I say.

She sets her cup down on the counter with a little more force than necessary. "What the hell is that meant to mean?"

"You've got the week off – it's all organised."

She scoffs. "Nice try, Andy. You don't even know where I work."

"Don't I?" I challenge.

"Nope." She smiles smugly at me.

I shrug. "Oh well then... I guess I *didn't* call into the office of 'The News Daily' after all... I didn't organise for you to have time off and I probably didn't get hit on by someone called *Stu* then either..."

Her jaw drops but she quickly recovers and snaps it shut.

"You *didn't*."

"Oh I did." I smirk. "Stu was more than happy to give you the rest of the week off – apparently you don't know how to relax and he thinks I'm just the man for the job." I puff my chest out proudly.

"I'll kill him," she states calmly. "He might be the best at digging up dirt and tracking people down, but I'll bury him so god damn deep even he won't be able to find himself."

I chuckle at her threat and shrug. "Whatever you say, princess, but it'll have to wait until next week – you're on holiday."

She crosses her arms across her chest – a stubborn-as-hell expression on her face. "I'm not going *anywhere* with you."

"Oh you'll come alright."

"That's what you think," she grumbles.

I stroll towards the door, fully clothed thanks to the ridiculous temperature she's still refusing to fix.

"Dylan?" I call when I'm just outside the doorway.

"*What*?" she snaps.

"I've still got my bike."

I don't miss the sound of her sharp intake of breath and muttered 'oh fuck'.

CHAPTER TWELVE

Dylan

"I'm not going because I want to spend time with *you*; I'm going because I want to see my girl. Just so we're clear." I jab a finger into his chest, so he knows I really mean business.

"Whatever helps you sleep at night." He smirks. "I know you just can't wait to wrap your legs around my waist again."

His words send goose bumps over my skin.

"Just open the door," I demand.

He squats down and undoes the lock on the door of the storage shed.

The door creaks as he lifts it up.

"There she is," he announces proudly.

There she is indeed. I might not be sure about much anymore, but I do know that I love that bike.

"She looks good," I murmur as I circle it, my fingers running lovingly over the dark leather and hard body.

"She got a full tune up," he says, sounding like a proud dad. "Still runs like a dream."

"You rode her without me?"

"You tried to *divorce* me. Of course I rode her without you."

I pout. "I think I missed this bike more than I missed you."

His lips break out into a smug grin. "So you *did* miss me."

"Don't twist my words."

"Just calling it as I see it." He chuckles. "Now put your helmet on, princess, we're getting the fuck out of here."

"Finally." I sigh dramatically. "He says something I *actually* want to hear."

He shakes his head in amusement and comes to stand in front of me, the helmet that was always mine in his hands.

He sits it on my head and then reaches under my chin to tighten up the strap.

His fingers brush my skin and make tingles race up and down my spine.

"Done," he murmurs softly.

"Thank you," I reply in the same way.

He gives me a smile that makes my stomach flutter and steps away from me.

I'm grateful for the space. We're about to get very up close and personal, and there will be no avoiding his hard, warm body, or that addictive scent once I'm on the back of his bike.

I've got no doubt that's why he brought me here.

After pulling that ridiculous stunt with my job that I'm sure Stu would have been all too eager to assist with, all bets are off. I know that now.

He's pulling out all the stops.

"You ready?" he asks, distracting me from my internal realisation.

He's sitting on the bike now and holy shit, if I wasn't totally screwed before, then I damn well am now.

He's every dream from the past three years come to life right in front of my eyes.

He looks like the Drew I fell in love with, and even though looks can be deceiving, I allow myself a moment to pretend that nothing has changed.

I let myself pretend that we're just Drew and Dylan – crazy in love with life and with each other.

I swing my leg over the back of the bike and snuggle into the leather jacket he's worn for the occasion, my legs clamping tightly around his hips.

"Hold on tight, princess."

My heart jackhammers in my chest.

It's what he's always said when I got on the back of his bike... ever since the very first time.

He didn't forget.

I know it's wrong of me, and that I shouldn't get either of our hopes up by repeating back my part of the line, but the words are out my mouth before I can convince myself it's a terrible idea.

"I'll never let go," I whisper.

I hear him exhale deeply before turning the key and making the bike roar to life.

I throw my head back and grin.

I've missed the purr of the Harley's engine something chronic.

I'd never even been on the back of a bike before Andy came crashing into my life and into my heart, but now I can barely imagine a time before I felt the freedom of the wind in my hair.

He pulls out of the shed carefully and before I know it, we're speeding off down an open road I've never travelled.

I don't know where he's taking me, but right now, I couldn't care less.

All that matters is that I'm here, with *him* of all people and I'm free.

I can pretend for a few hours that the last three years never even happened.

I can be the woman in love with her husband without having to hide it or feel ashamed of the fact.

Andy yells something to me over his shoulder that I don't catch, but I don't care. I just grin and press the side of my face into his back as I cling on tight.

I never imagined myself on the back of a bike, but I feel free out here. I trust him on this thing in a way I'm not sure I could trust another person.

After what feels like forever, the bike starts to slow, before leaving the sealed road entirely and driving onto a bumpy, gravel track.

He has to drive a lot slower now, and the noise is lower, low enough that I can talk to him.

"Where are we?" I ask.

"You'll see in about five minutes," he calls back over his shoulder.

I take a good look around now that things aren't passing in such a blur. We're in a totally secluded, rural-looking part of the countryside. I can't see a single sign of life out here other than a few odd cattle grazing in a nearby paddock.

There's a thick cover of bush that we're approaching, and I should probably be worried that my convict husband is going to murder me and dump my body in the woods, but I'm not.

I know Andy would never hurt me, not physically anyway.

He might have done a lot of questionable things since the day I met him and long before that too, but I know I can trust him to keep me safe from harm. He'd kill anyone or anything that tried to hurt me.

I know he'd die for me if he had to.

We drive into the bush and I'm struck with just how beautiful it is out here. The trees almost cover the sky entirely with green.

It's like we've been transported into some type of wild jungle.

Andy pulls the bike to a stop and flicks down the stand with his foot.

Turning to face me, he announces, "Here we are."

I pull off my helmet as he climbs off the bike.

He offers me his hand to help me get off and I try my hardest not to think words like 'sweet' or 'charming' about him.

Words like that aren't going to end well for my self-control.

"What is this place?" I ask him as I look around in bewilderment.

He's still got hold of my hand, but I let him keep it. Besides the fact that I like the feel of it, I need it too, I have no idea where I am or where we're going.

I'm a city girl – bush land isn't exactly my comfort zone.

"I found this place by accident," he tells me. "The minute I got out, I got on my bike and just drove."

We're walking now, strolling along hand in hand as he talks.

"I've never felt so free, Dylan, I just drove until I got to a dead end."

He pulls me out of the bush and into a clearing and I gasp.

It's *beautiful*.

We're at the edge of a huge riverbed.

There's a waterfall pounding over the drop further upstream and into the huge swimming hole in front of us.

The cliff face is covered in greenery and wildflowers and I've seriously never seen anything so pure or untouched in my whole life.

"Wow," I breathe.

"Can you imagine coming from something like a cage, to *this*?"

I shake my head.

"I needed it, even I didn't know how much, Dylan. I was going mad in there. It wasn't until I got out that I realised I hadn't really breathed for three years."

He tugs me along until we reach a couple of huge rocks. He sits down on one and pats the spot next to him, indicating that I should sit too.

And like the total sucker I am, I do.

"So you came straight here?" I ask.

It's not like I probably deserved it, but I'd thought he would have come looking for me. The man I fell in love with would have always looked for me first. *No matter what.*

He must hear the question I'm not saying because he answers it.

"I went to our house first," he replies tightly. "You weren't there."

I don't answer – there's nothing I can say, and not a day goes by that I don't wish I didn't sell the home we built together, but it just had to be done.

Good choices aren't always easy ones.

"So then I just drove. I tried to leave all my problems in my rear-view mirror, but it didn't work."

"It didn't?"

He shakes his head. "Even something this incredible doesn't compare to what I lost when you walked out of my life."

I shiver at the honesty in his words.

He's vulnerable Andy again – and I'm totally and utterly defenceless.

He takes my hand in his and once more, I let him.

He rubs his thumb over the shiny gold polish on my long nails before bringing the back of my hand to his lips and kissing it gently.

"Fuck, I missed you, Dylan, every god damn second of every single day."

I missed you too. I want to reply, but I can't. I have to protect myself.

"You got out early," I say instead.

"Good behaviour." He nods.

"*You*?" I tease. "I didn't know you knew the meaning of it."

"I would have done anything to get out of there early, princess – even behave myself."

I smile sadly at him. I feel sorry for him, even though I know I shouldn't. I never have been able to handle seeing him sad.

"Three years of my life, princess... it's just gone."

Three years of my life is gone too – not in the same way – I know he's had a hard time, but I have too. He knows nothing of the torture I've lived through while he was away.

I shrug. "What did you expect would happen when you broke the law?"

He doesn't answer me, we just sit in silence for a long, long moment.

I'm not sure when it happened, but by the time he speaks again I realise my eyes are closed and my head is resting on his shoulder.

"I *didn't* do it," he whispers to me.

My heart speeds up to a thunderous pace in my chest as I lift my head.

"You didn't do *what*?" I ask, even though I know exactly what he's talking about.

"I didn't steal that bike, Dylan." His gorgeous brown eyes are overflowing with sincerity.

It's so intense I have to look away to catch my breath.

"They caught you driving it," I reply quickly.

The facts were all there. I may not have visited him or sat in the court room myself, but I saw every single bit of the case against him.

"Doesn't mean I stole it." He shrugs.

I don't reply. I *can't*; my head is swirling so fast I feel like I could pass out.

I don't know what to do with this information.

The old me would have believed him in a heartbeat.

He wasn't kidding when he swore he'd never lied to me. Other than this whole saga, I've never heard a single word of a lie come from his lips.

But he can't be telling the truth now. He just *can't*.

He went to prison over this.

I *left* him over this.

"I didn't do any of it. I didn't operate that business. I didn't steal any of those vehicles."

My husband was sentenced to four and half years for grand theft auto. They accused him of running an illegal operation – stealing cars and bikes and flipping them for quick sale.

It could have been a lot more time, but he got lucky – there wasn't a lot in the way of solid evidence to tie him to the entire operation, so instead they stung him hard with what they could – the stolen bike he was caught on.

"You worked on *all* of those cars, Andy. Every single one they seized had your prints on it."

He drops his head. "I know I did. And I knew there was something dodgy going down, but the money was good, *too* good for a guy working based on commission, so I didn't ask any questions and I paid the price for it."

We paid the price for it, I think to myself, but I don't say it aloud.

"You never told me about any of this, why?"

He shrugs. "What's to tell? A lot of cars came through the garage, princess, it just so happened that about half of them came from one man."

"*Andy.*" I look at him sceptically. "They never found a man."

I read his statement. Someone called '*Terry*' was who Andy blamed. He knew nothing more about the man and the police never found any trace of someone by that name.

"I'm not lying to you, Dylan. Why the fuck would I? I did the time. It's done. I can't get it back. Whether or not I'm guilty is pretty god damn irrelevant right now."

"It's not to me," I whisper.

"You think I'm lying anyway," he mutters as his brown eyes search mine.

"I looked at the facts."

"Fuck the facts. You know me, princess, a man that kisses you like that isn't lying to you – you know that."

"A man that kisses me like what?" I breathe – terrified about what I know is going to come next.

"Like *this*," he growls as he reaches for me and pulls my face to his.

I don't even fight him – instead I welcome it.

I allow myself to be the old Dylan for yet another second.

I allow myself to believe that my husband didn't do the very thing that caused us to fall apart.

I allow myself to give in to him the way I've wanted to since the first moment I laid eyes on him again.

He runs his tongue along my bottom lip and I open my mouth for him.

His tongue finds mine, seeking entry gently, and I moan.

My noises only spur him on further and before I even know what's happening, I'm being lifted into his lap, straddling him in a position that's all too familiar.

My hands are in his hair and his are on my waist, his fingers digging into my flesh, but I still don't feel close enough.

It's electric, this moment. I can almost feel the crackle in the air between us.

"*Drew*," I moan as I nip at his bottom lip.

"Jesus, Dylan." He pants as his hand slides up my body to cup my face.

We're both breathing heavily, like we've been for a long run, our breaths mingling together as he places random kisses on my face.

The corner of my mouth, my brow, my cheek, my forehead...

He's kissing me all over.

I giggle as he kisses the skin below my ear.

"Making up for lost time," he growls as he kisses the same spot again.

I sigh and let my eyelids flutter shut.

I can't live in this moment for long, I know that, but I'm not willing to give it up just yet – it's too good.

"You don't believe me," he whispers hoarsely against my ear.

"I don't know what I believe anymore," I whisper back with total honesty, the words surprising even myself.

CHAPTER THIRTEEN

Andy

I don't want to get cocky, but it feels like I've got my wife back.

I know there's still a long road ahead, but today has been one hell of a baby step for both of us.

She didn't run when I kissed her – not that she would have got far out here in the countryside, not in those tight-as-fuck pants anyway – but the point is, she didn't even *try* to run.

She wanted to be here as much as I did, and that's saying something.

I've fantasised about this moment for a long time. I didn't think I'd actually get it.

I'm free – driving my bike with the woman of my dreams wrapped around me like a vice and I've never been a happier man.

We're driving aimlessly, both of us just enjoying the ride, and wherever it is we're headed, I know this is the direction I want to take for the rest of my life.

I'll go *anywhere* as long as it's with her.

Things with Dylan were never going to be a sprint – even calling it a marathon doesn't seem enough of an effort – no offence to those crazy bastards who run those things – but I know this is going to take a lot more out of me than any run ever could.

I know it's going to take me a long time to fix what I broke between us.

Even though I didn't do what I was accused of, I left myself wide open to taking the blame.

I might not have been guilty, but it was still my fault that I had to leave her.

I was young and naive and it's not a mistake I'll be making again.

I'd be lying if I said it didn't hurt me that she never came to me, never asked for my side of the story – because it did. It crushed me.

I saw the look in her eyes as she watched me being put in the back of that cop car.

She went from looking like the happiest I'd ever seen her, to looking like she had died inside.

I'll never forget that look.

It was the sight of me breaking the person I loved most in the world. The only person I've ever loved more than myself.

I feel her tug on the sleeve of my jacket and I glance back at her over my shoulder as I slow to a stop at an intersection.

We've ended up two towns over in some little hick village I've never been to.

"You okay, princess?"

I'm expecting her to ask me to take her home, I've been waiting for it all day, but she doesn't.

"I'm hungry," she says instead.

I chuckle. "Of course you are."

She smacks my arm teasingly. "Just feed me already."

"Yes, ma'am."

***

"So, were you in some kinda gang?" She tips her head to the side as she studies me carefully.

She's onto her fourth or so beer and she's close to being pissed already.

Dylan might be able to eat me under the table, but she's a complete lightweight on the drink.

I chuckle. "No. I wasn't in a fucking gang."

"Did you join a fight club?"

"And mess up this pretty face?" I smirk at her. "What do you think?"

She bites down on her lip as her green eyes linger on my face. "*Such* a pretty face." She sighs dreamily.

I chuckle again. She's definitely drunk.

"I got out early on good behaviour, princess, remember? That doesn't work if you're joining gangs and beating the crap out of some piece-of-shit jail trash."

She almost looks a little bit disappointed.

"Were you anyone's bitch?" She giggles.

"Do I look like the kinda guy who's gonna be someone's bitch?"

Her eyes widen. "Oh shit, did you make someone *your* bitch?"

I laugh long and loud.

"No, Dylan, don't worry, Jesus, I kept my dick to myself." She blushes, and I wink at her. "I was saving it for you."

She rolls her eyes.

"I did make a couple of mates in there, though."

"Oh yeah? I bet they're really upstanding citizens," she drawls as she brings her beer bottle up to her lips and takes a long drink.

Fuck she looks too good doing that.

We're going to have to get the hell out of this shitty little pub soon, before I end up giving the other patrons a show they're not likely to forget.

She raises her brows at me and I realise she's waiting for me to speak.

"Ah..." I clear my throat. "Yeah, they're good dudes."

"Good dudes that are behind bars for *what* exactly?"

"Robbo's locked up for producing fake documents – passports and stuff, and Glow, he has a fetish for lighting shit on fire. He got caught burning down an old abandoned church or some shit."

"Charming."

"They actually kinda were. There's some real bad dudes in there, princess. It was no maximum security, but some of those hopped-up little punks would have stabbed their grandma for five bucks. So, all things considered, these two were pretty good guys."

She twirls a strand of red hair around her finger as she watches me talk. "They still in there?"

"The hopped-up punks?" I question.

"*Your boys*," she elaborates with a hint of a slur in her voice.

"Glow got out six months before me and Robbo will be out early next year if he can keep his nose clean."

"Drugs?" she asks with a solemn nod.

I chuckle. "There's plenty in there, but nah, it's just an expression, princess – he just needs to stay out of trouble."

"Got it." She takes the final pull of her beer and looks at me with a sleepy smile.

"We better get the hell outta here before you fall asleep."

She doesn't reply as I stand up and throw some money on the table to cover the bill. I take her hand and tow her along beside me.

"And before you ask, I didn't do drugs in there."

"Were they not good drugs?" she asks as she snuggles into my side.

I throw my arm around her and help her walk straight.

I'm doing my best not to laugh at her, I really am, but there's nothing much funnier than Dylan when she's crossed the line from drunk to too drunk. She can go from full noise to sleepy puppy in about thirty seconds flat.

"No, baby, they were shit drugs."

I manage to get the helmet on her head and her sexy ass onto the bike, but I'm not entirely convinced she's going to be able to stay awake to hold on.

She's wearing a scarf so I take it off from around her neck as she sits there looking at me with a dopey smile on her face.

I get on and with more effort than I was fucking prepared for, I get the scarf wrapped around both of us and tie it up at the front so she's attached to me.

Last thing I need is her falling off. That's not going to win me any points.

"I gotta get that car finished," I mutter to myself and she wraps her arms around my waist.

"What are you waiting for, fire her up," Dylan slurs, waving one hand around in some obscene gesture.

I start my baby up with a chuckle and head for home.

I don't know how long Dylan lasts before she nods off, but when I park the bike up outside her apartment, she's asleep.

***

I creep out of the bedroom and pull the door shut behind me.

The woman still sleeps like the dead.

I carried her up here, got her into bed, stripped her pants off – and she only woke once. Even then, all she did was smile up at me and mutter the word, '*Drew*'.

Fucking *heartbreaker*.

I'd give anything to be *Drew* for her again. I'm not all about emotions and feelings or any of that shit, but I'd be lying if I said that hearing my name from her lips doesn't stir something up inside me.

I drop down onto the couch and shiver.

It's still fucking freezing in this place and I'm going to have to do something about it soon.

I grab my phone and scroll through my contacts, hitting call when I get to Jeff's name.

"Wood," he answers after a few rings.

"What's going on? Everything all good at work?"

"It's good. Just left the garage. How's the wife? Still hate your guts?"

It's an interesting question, and one I'm not really sure how to answer. I know she doesn't exactly like me yet, but she didn't seem to hate me quite so much today either.

"A bit less... I think."

"You think she's warming up to you?"

I chuckle. "Ironic choice of words... She cut off the heating in here. I'm freezing my ass off."

"Why'd she do that for?"

"I refused to wear clothes."

He chuckles down the line. "That's gold. I really do love that woman. I hope you don't fuck this up. I'd like having her around again."

"Yeah well I'd hate to let you down," I drawl sarcastically.

"You getting anywhere with her?"

"I kissed her. She didn't bail."

"Solid."

"We took my bike for a ride."

He chuckles. "You softened her up with the Harley, that's sly, man, I like it."

"We had dinner in some dive pub, it was... like old times."

"Why the fuck are you talking to me instead of her then?"

"She had about half a dozen beers."

"*Right*," he acknowledges. "She out to it?"

"Dead to the world."

"Same old lightweight Dylan." He chuckles.

"The very one."

"What have you got up your sleeve for tomorrow?"

"I dunno, man, I just want to survive it without making her cry again," I mutter.

"You made her cry?" he demands.

He sounds more like an angry older brother than a concerned friend, but I don't even bother arguing with him about his tone. If I fuck this thing up with Dylan, I won't need him to kick my ass, I'll do it myself.

"Yesterday. I dunno what the fuck I did, Stonesie, she went to sleep crying and then woke up like it never happened."

"Women are baffling creatures, Wood."

"Not Dylan. She's not one of those girls who hides things and talks in circles."

"She might not have been that girl before, but you don't know who she is now," he replies quietly.

I get the feeling he knows something he's not telling me. So I ask him a question I haven't asked since I first got locked up.

"Did you talk to her while I was gone?"

He blows out a breath. "Once, man, just once."

"You didn't tell me," I growl.

"She asked me not to."

"Well that's fucking great, you're *my* mate, Jeff – mine."

"I'm her friend too," he snaps. "Just because she didn't want to know you anymore doesn't mean she couldn't talk to me. I tried to call her every day for three months, Wood. I wanted to help her, but she wouldn't let me. You're not the only one she shut out."

It hits me then, just how much damage has been done. Not only to me, but to those closest to me.

I don't know if any of us will ever be the same again.

"Fuck, I'm sorry." I blow out a breath.

He sighs. "I know you are, man."

"We good?"

"Of course we're fucking good."

There's silence for a beat.

"So when did you talk to her?"

"It was a about a month or two after you went in. She called me out of the blue on a private line. She asked me if you were okay."

"That's it?"

"That's it."

"What did you tell her?"

"I told her that you'd been better, but that you'd be fine. I told her you'd get out one day and when that day came, you'd try and get her back – so she better be ready."

"What did she say to that?"

"She hung up on me. Never heard from her again until she called me up and bowled into the garage the other day."

"I'm really trying to get her back, Jeff. I want it so bad."

"I know you do, Wood, just stick at it. She'll come around."

"I told her I was innocent."

"She believe you?"

I think about it for a minute.

"I'm not sure she wants to have her mind changed... you know how stubborn she is. She saw the facts back then and that was enough for her."

"Then maybe it's time you looked for some new facts."

CHAPTER FOURTEEN

Dylan

I blink drowsily and groan as the light from the open curtain hits me right in the eyes.

"Make it stop," I grumble.

I reach around without thinking and then freeze when I realise what I'm doing.

I'm feeling for Andy in the space next to me.

I groan again, this time out of frustration at myself.

This week of 'married bliss' is not going to plan at all.

He's wearing me down, and fast. At this rate I'll be asking him to sleep with me after all, and then I'll be completely screwed – if I'm not already.

I'll never be able to give him up if I let him into my pants.

I roll over and my senses are assaulted with the smell of him on my sheets. I breathe in deeply, inhaling every little bit of him that I can.

It's just me in here – no one can see me being weak and stupid, and if no one sees, then it doesn't count.

That's my new motto anyway.

He's definitely been in here again – not that I would have even bothered to tell him no if he'd asked. The half-cut state I was in, I probably would have been begging him to stay with me.

I roll back over and throw the covers off myself, and it's only then that I realise I'm only in my top and underwear.

I grimace.

I'm ninety-nine percent sure I didn't do anything more than sleep last night, but there's still that one percent of uncertainty I'm looking to squash.

My eyes scan the room until I find the pants I was wearing last night, folded neatly on my dresser.

I breathe a sigh of relief. Now I'm one hundred percent safe.

Andy isn't the kind of man who folds up your clothes before fucking your brains out. No, he's the bastard who barely manages to leave any item of clothing in one piece as he rips it from your body – no matter how expensive it was.

There was no sex happening in this room last night – not any that involved me at least.

"Andy?" I call out.

There's no reply.

I grab the water off the bedside table and take a swig of it.

I don't know if I'm hungover or what, but it feels hot in here. Like, super hot.

I roll out of bed and pad across the room, not even bothering to put on my pants.

Andy's clearly seen everything last night anyway, and who knows, maybe it might give me the upper hand in this power struggle we've got going on if I take a leaf out of his book of seduction.

I walk out into the hallway and I'm hit by a wave of heat so strong I consider turning back around and dialling for help.

I *definitely* did not imagine it.

It's like a sauna in here.

"Andy?" I yell.

I'm becoming more and more concerned by the second that his new cooking skills have gone wrong and he's about to burn the entire building to the ground.

"In here, princess," he calls back.

I follow the sound of his voice to the living room where I find him sitting on the couch. No flames – no raging inferno.

He's back wearing only his usual boxer briefs, although this pair is grey, a backwards baseball cap and absolutely nothing else.

He's got one arm slung over the back of the couch and the other inside his boxers.

That's when I figure out what he's done. The bastard has played me at my own game.

"Oh Jesus, you *didn't*."

"I did." He smirks. "Might be too hot to wear anything at all." He grins smugly.

"It's about *one thousand* degrees in here," I whine.

"It's a fucking upgrade from the freezer, is what it is."

"My power bill is going to be outrageous." I sigh in defeat.

I should have known better than to start a war with him.

He's better at it than I am.

"Come watch the replay of the game with me." He gestures towards the T.V.

I take a minute to really look at him. He might have technically won this round, but it's not like all is lost.

He's quite the sight.

I pause for a minute, debating my options before tugging my own top over my head, revealing the black lace bra I'm wearing, that matches my black boy-leg underwear.

I'm not a particularly confident woman when it comes to my body, I've always thought I've had a bit too much ass, tits and thighs, but those insecurities never followed me into my relationship with Andy. He's always made me feel like I'm the sexiest woman in the room.

I toss my shirt onto the chair and stroll over to sit next to him on the couch. "What are we watching?"

He doesn't answer me so I glance over at him. His eyes are almost popping out of his head.

"What?' I ask innocently. "It's hot in here."

He groans and lets his head fall back. "Okay, you win... *fu-uuuck*... I'll put the temperature back."

"Nah leave it, we'll split the bill." I wink at him.

"Leave it?" he mutters. "*Sweet baby Jesus.*"

I laugh. "What's the matter, you can't handle a woman in her underwear anymore?"

"I've spent the past three years surrounded by about four hundred men," he growls like he's almost in pain. "What the hell do you think?"

"Well you should have thought about that before you made this place a tropical paradise and tried to out play me."

I put my feet up on the coffee table and make a show of watching the game.

He tries to focus on the T.V, he really does, but I see his eyes darting back to look at me every few seconds.

"You can't sit there like that, princess."

"Why not?" I ask without looking at him.

"I can't handle it. I'm like a jacked-up teenager with too much time on my hands and a full load to blow."

I can feel the corner of my mouth twitching with a grin, but I do everything in my power to keep it locked down.

"Maybe you should get your hand out of your pants, I doubt all that fiddling is doing you any favours."

I glance pointedly at his crotch and then back at the screen in front of us.

"I'm holding it down, Dylan," he groans. "The visiting team's score won't be the only thing that's up if I let go now."

That comment pushes me over the edge and I erupt into laughter.

"You're such a boy." I giggle as he continues to stare at me with a pained glance.

I've got no doubt he's being serious, and the idea of me turning him on to this extent is doing wonders for my self-esteem.

"I'd argue with you, but right now, I feel a lot like a little boy." He shakes his head in disgust at himself.

His eyes rake over my body once again and this time I feel them.

Goose bumps break out on every surface of bare skin on my body under his intense watch.

I might have the upper hand right now, but I have a feeling I'm about to pass it over in favour of being flat on my back.

"You ready to tell me you're giving up the no sex rule yet?" he asks, his voice sounding like gravel.

I shake my head unconvincingly.

"You sure, princess?"

I'm not sure about *anything* anymore. I'm not sure if my husband is a thief, or if he's innocent. I'm not sure if I want a divorce, or if I want to stay married. I'm not sure if I want to run away from him right now, or if I want to throw myself at him...

I don't know shit about shit.

"Dylan, I—" he begins to say, but he's cut off by the sound of keys turning in the lock on my door.

"Oh no," I mutter.

There's only one person who has a key to my house and that's Sarah. And what she's about to walk into is not going to look good.

"Cover yourself up," I hiss as I throw the closest thing I can reach to him – a cushion. "Right now."

"*What*?" he asks in confusion.

"Fuck a duck why is it so hot in here?" she yells.

I turn and shoot her a sheepish smile over my shoulder as she gets a good look at the scene in front of her.

"Well, well, well, this isn't something you see every day..." She smirks as she looks at the pair of us.

CHAPTER FIFTEEN

Andy

"It pains me to say it, Andrew, but you're looking fantastic."

Her eyes are looking me over shamelessly, and I'm not surprised, Sarah is a *painfully* honest, big mouthed, sharp shooter of a woman. She says everything that she thinks. She's never made any secret of her appreciation for my physique or her more recent distaste for me in general.

Sarah's been like a little sister to me since the day I met her – albeit a pervy little sister – but she's always been the biggest cheerleader for me and Dylan.

She could see I made her best friend happy and that was all it took for her to decide she wanted to be on team Dylan and Andy.

It's different now than it was then, and I know damn well that if I'm going to earn forgiveness from my wife, then I'm going to have to make it up to her best friend too.

These two are a package deal everywhere except the bedroom.

"I see you haven't changed a bit, Sarah," I say.

"Not that I'm complaining, but what's with the heat and no clothes?" She glances back and forth between the two of us for an answer.

"I'll fill you in later," Dylan tells her.

"Even better, you can fill me in *now*, our coffee date doesn't change because of Mr. striped jumpsuit over here, right?"

"It's my late-start day; we get coffee every Wednesday morning..." Dylan explains and looks at me expectantly.

I realise she's waiting for me to tell her to go.

"Oh, go ahead," I encourage. "You can keep falling in love with me again when you get back."

Dylan blushes and Sarah narrows her eyes at me.

"I've got a few calls to make anyway," I say.

Sarah gestures for me to go ahead and get up and I nod in acceptance.

I'm going to have to do the walk of shame.

The only positive about her turning up here is that it sorted out the issue in my pants really fucking quick.

Sarah is an attractive woman, but she's scary as hell.

Scary enough to send me limp in about two seconds flat.

"Well, Sarah, thanks for the eye fuck." I nod at her.

I lean over and kiss Dylan – who's put her shirt back on – on the forehead. "I'll see you in a couple of hours, princess."

I get up and head for the hallway with my head held high. No sooner am I out of sight that I hear them.

"Oh you are *so* fucked! Head kisses, '*princess*'... Jesus, did you see the ass on him? Christ, you're not getting out of this alive, D, I can tell you that much for nothing."

I chuckle and hope like hell that Sarah is right about that.

***

"Hello, Stuart speaking," the voice on the other end of the line answers.

"Hey, Stu, this is Andrew Woodman, I met with you a few days ago?"

"I remember," he says. "My little DD's stud muffin of a husband."

"Did you just say stud muffin?"

"Mmm hmm," he replies.

I chuckle. "Alright then."

"What can I do for you, Mr. *Wood*man?"

I do my best to ignore his flirty tone and sexual innuendos, "I was actually hoping you could help me with something. Dylan told me that you're the man to see if you want to dig up some dirt."

"You want me to find the person who sat back and watched you take the fall, am I right?"

I'm pacing the room and when he speaks I falter mid-step.

"How'd you know that?"

"I'm just *that* good."

I chuckle, almost nervously.

I never told him anything about going to prison or that I was innocent.

So, either Dylan's been talking about me... or...

"You dug up my dirt, didn't you?" I question him.

"Oh, honey, every last little bit of it."

"Why?"

"Wifey's request."

"Huh," I muse. "*Interesting.*"

"Not as interesting as your past there, muscles... a stunt in juvey for repeated dangerous driving, more speeding fines than you can shake a dick at..."

"Uh, I think the saying is 'shake a stick at,'" I point out.

"Not in this office it's not." He retorts suggestively.

I can't help but laugh. He's totally inappropriate and I like that about him.

Life's too short to be boring.

"I was seventeen," I explain. "I was a punk-ass little kid."

"And what exactly are you now?" he prompts.

"Now I'm a slightly less punk-ass twenty-something-year-old."

"With a rap sheet to match."

"A rap sheet for something I didn't do."

He's silent for a moment.

"I never thought you did."

"*Why*?" I ask as I breathe out a sigh of relief – if he believes me, he might help me, and right now I need all the help I can get.

"You pled not guilty when you could have pled guilty and taken a deal, there's nothing solid linking you to any of the cars except the prints, but you're a mechanic, so duh... and most importantly you're just too pretty to be a thief."

I shake my head in amusement. "I worked on the cars – but I didn't steal them, or flip them, for that matter."

"And the five-hundred-thousand-dollar, *stolen* motorcycle they caught you on?" he questions.

"It was a five-hundred-thousand-dollar motorcycle," I repeat back to him. "I gave it a service and took it for a joy ride."

"That was smart," he says sarcastically.

"It was a *five-hundred-thousand-dollar motorcycle*," I say again. "I was a twenty-three-year-old petrol head with a fetish for things that go fast – of course I took it for a spin... I test run every vehicle that comes in; how am I meant to know if I fixed the fucking thing otherwise?"

"Don't ask me, handsome."

"You gotta take that baby for a ride... but maybe this was a slightly extended, faster ride... can you blame a guy?"

"So it was just wrong place, wrong time?"

"I guess so."

"Or you were set up."

"I doubt it. The bike was reported stolen and I was driving it like I'd done exactly that. But either way, I took a ride in a cop car that didn't come back again, and whoever was actually running the show got off free and easy – albeit slightly inconvenienced."

"Did you know they raided a warehouse about an hour's drive from the garage you worked in? They found over thirty vehicles in there – all of them with your prints under the hoods."

"I heard. They wanted me to confess to running it all."

The cops couldn't tie me to the actual warehouse itself – that's the only reason I didn't get more time.

They uncovered a major operation and they wanted to hold someone responsible – I just so happened to be that scapegoat when they had no luck finding the man who was really in charge.

"Who brought the cars to you?"

"Someone called Terry."

I hear him jotting down notes.

"That's it? No last name?"

"Bro, I doubt that was even his first name," I drawl. "And good luck finding anything at all about him, the guy's like a ghost, *trust me*, I've had people try."

"Well you haven't had *me*. And like your sexy little wifey said, I'm the *best*."

CHAPTER SIXTEEN

Dylan

"You look happy." Sarah observes as she sips on her double shot. She's much more relaxed now that she's got some caffeine running through her veins.

I almost felt sorry for Andy earlier, feeling the wrath of Sarah before she's had her coffee is not something I'd wish upon anyone – not even the man who broke my heart.

"I don't want to feel happy," I admit sheepishly, "but you know what he's always done to me."

"So are you going to take him back then?" she asks. There's judgement in her voice, but a lot of curiosity.

I close my eyes and take a deep breath.

It's the million-dollar question.

Even after all these years I still feel *everything* when he's near.

But it's a risk – *he's* a risk – and it's one I'm not sure I'm willing to take yet.

"You don't even know, do you?" she prompts me.

I shake my head. "He told me he didn't steal that bike, Sare."

She sighs. "Of course he said that, he'd say *anything* to get you back, you know that."

"I know..." I nod. "I *know* he would, but can you honestly think of an instance where he's lied to me? Even just *one*? Because I can't..."

"That time out at the lake when he told you he could hold his breath under water for two minutes?" she offers.

"He nearly drowned trying." I cackle at the memory. "Stupid fool really thought he could do it."

She laughs before quieting down and shaking her head. "I can't, D. He's always been honest with you," she admits.

"That's what I'm afraid of."

"Why?" Her voice is soft and probing.

"What if I left him for nothing?" I whisper.

She reaches across, takes my hand and gives it a squeeze – she understands my guilt.

"I'm sure he'll understand why you did what you did. And even if he wasn't running the show with those cars, he's not an idiot, Dylan – contrary to what I might have called him over the years – he must have known *something* was going on, and he didn't say a word about it... that's on him, not you."

She might be right, but it doesn't help my guilt.

"He might not be as guilty as we thought... *maybe* – and that's a big maybe, but either way he's not entirely innocent either, don't you forget that."

"Yeah... I guess you might be right."

"I'm *always* right."

She watches me as she sips on her coffee.

"I don't know what to do, Sare."

She shrugs. "Do you think that maybe you should try giving him a real shot and see what happens?"

My jaw drops at her suggestion. "Unless you mean with a gun, I'm not sure I believe what I'm hearing."

She huffs out a laugh and holds her hands up in a gesture of surrender. "I know, I know... but I've seen what you're up against now... and *dammmmn*, I can't believe you haven't let him blow out the cobwebs yet – you're a stronger woman than I am, that's for damn sure."

"Right?" I breathe. "I *told* you he'd got even better looking."

"They should put him on a calendar or something, it's just ridiculous."

"I'd pay good money for that."

"Newsflash, honey, you don't have to pay, you can get all of that for *free*."

I feel like laughing and crying at the same time.

It's all so complicated when it used to be so simple.

We met, fell in love, got married and started to build a life together. All within the space of about eight months... it was fast, but it was real.

There was drama – there always is, but we loved each other. That much was certain.

He really is the only man I've ever been able to envision having a life with – the minute he spoke to me and looked at me with those warm brown eyes, he curled his way around my heart, and I've never been able to vacate him from his spot.

I want to let him in again, I *do*, but I'm scared. We're strangers in a sense now – there's so much we don't know about the other anymore.

There's so much to learn all over again.

Deep down, I know that I probably still know all the important stuff – it's like riding a bike... you don't just forget it, but there's parts of him I don't know at all, and that terrifies me.

There are so many days and nights that he's had without me by my side, and that thought alone threatens to crush me.

I vowed to spend every minute of the rest of my life loving this man, and although I've never stopped loving him, I stopped showing him that love.

I broke my promise.

"Have you told him, D?" Sarah coaxes. "Because maybe it's time you did."

Ice slides slowly down my spine, like someone has literally taken an ice cube and run it down the entire length of my back.

I haven't told him anything real.

"I don't know how," I whisper.

She nods in understanding. "When the time is right, you'll figure out a way."

"He'll be so angry."

"No, he'll be heartbroken," she insists.

"I'm not sure that's any better."

I can feel my face paling at just the thought of having this conversation. I feel physically ill.

"If you can consider overlooking his stint in jail, I think he'll be able to get through anything you tell him."

It's what we promised each other all those years ago – he always said there was nothing we couldn't get through if we were together. I just have to hope that he was right about something after all.

"I don't know..." I sigh.

"I'm *always* right, remember? Just let him in. Give it a go, D, worry about everything else when you have to, okay?"

The thought of letting my guard down and letting Andy in feels like the most right thing in the world.

I want us to have a chance.

I stand up slowly. "You know what? I think maybe I should go home now."

She smiles at me. "I think that's a good idea."

Suddenly I can't get out of there fast enough.

"Hey, D?" she calls, and I stop in my tracks and turn back around to hear what she has to say.

"I know I haven't been his biggest fan these past few years, but I just want to see you happy. If Andy makes you happy, then you should be with him – regardless of what anyone thinks."

"Thanks, Sare." I try to swallow the lump that has formed in my throat.

"And one more thing..." she adds quickly before I have a chance to escape again. "If he says he didn't do it... I'm inclined to believe him. That man *never* lies to you."

CHAPTER SEVENTEEN

Andy

"I was starting to think you weren't coming home, princess."

She shoots me a sheepish look as she shuts the front door behind her.

She eyes me up and down and her eyebrows raise in surprise. "You're fully dressed."

I chuckle. "I put the heat back to normal... I felt a bit dirty after your friend eye fucked me."

She doesn't walk into the room like I expect her to, instead she leans her back against the closed door and watches me.

"Same old Sarah." She giggles nervously.

I don't know what went down on their little coffee date, but it's clear that something has changed.

Dylan doesn't seem as guarded. She's afraid, even terrified maybe, but in a good way – like she's about to take a risk on something.

I hope like fuck that risk is me.

"How was your morning?" I ask her.

She blushes a light pink on her cheeks that makes me want to ask her one hundred more questions, but I don't.

"It was... good... *insightful*..."

I smirk at her. "Insightful?"

"Yeah." She smiles at me and my heart thuds in my chest. "Insightful."

The power of that smile has never worn off. It still controls me the same way it always has.

I'd do just about anything to see one of those smiles on her pretty face.

"You're talking in code, princess." I cross my arms across my chest and watch her with interest.

I don't know what she's thinking right now and as much as the unknown intrigues me, it scares me too.

"What are we doing for the rest of the day?" she surprises me by asking.

"You're willingly going to spend the afternoon with me?"

She nods coyly.

"Who are you and what the fuck did you do with my wife?" I demand with a grin.

She giggles again and runs her hand through her long red hair.

She doesn't even deny being my wife, in fact, she doesn't say a thing at all.

She just stands there, looking at me with bright, excited eyes, and all of a sudden, I can't take the space between us anymore.

I cross the room and press my body against hers, resting each of my hands against the door near her head.

I'm surrounding her, yet she seems totally at ease with the closeness.

This isn't the same Dylan from three days ago – this is the old Dylan. *My* Dylan.

"You've been thinking about what I said," I state.

"I have."

"Do you believe me?" I growl the words at her, not realising just how important the answer to this question is to me until I say it aloud.

"The jury's still out," she whispers.

I nod my head in acceptance.

It's not a yes, but it's not a no either and that's a fucking win in my book.

"I'm going to prove it to you, princess."

She looks me right in the eye and nods her head. "Okay."

I can feel my heart thumping against my ribcage as she utters the single word.

This is a *big* moment for us.

She's letting me in.

"Yeah?"

"Yeah."

She reaches slowly up with her hands and clasps my face.

"I missed you when you were gone," she whispers, so, so, quietly.

I feel like I'm in a dream, like I'm going to wake up any minute now and none of this will have really happened.

I don't recall falling asleep while I waited for her – but this seems too good to be true.

"Am I dreaming?" I ask her as she pushes her hands into my hair, her arms resting on my shoulders.

"I hope not." She giggles. "I drove around for an hour trying to find the courage to say that to you, and I really don't want to have to do it again."

I wrap my arms around her middle and pull her against me as tight as I can.

Holding her is something so simple, but it's something I wasn't sure I'd ever get the chance to do again, so I revel in the feeling of it – I drown myself in her.

"Fuck I missed you, Dylan."

"You told me." She sniffs.

I pull back so I can look at her.

She's crying and my heart sinks in my chest.

"Princess, what's wrong?"

She shakes her head and swipes at the tears trailing down her face. "I'm scared, Andy."

"Scared of what?" I coax as I wipe her cheeks dry.

"Of us."

"Don't be. I'm not scared of us," I tell her softly.

"You're not?" She looks up at me with wide, vulnerable eyes.

This is the moment when I need to think about what I say and not just blurt out the first scrap of bullshit that rolls through my thick head.

She's craving the man I keep beneath the layers of ego and armour, and if I want my wife back like this – in my arms and in my life, I'm going to have to let him out more often.

"No." I shake my head. "I'm only scared of *you*, Dylan. You're the only one with any real power to hurt me."

"I don't want to hurt you," she whispers. "Hurting you would hurt me too."

I glance over my shoulder in the direction of the dining table and more importantly, the stack of papers on top of it.

"I'm scared of those papers," I admit.

"Forget the papers for now," she whispers.

"Yeah?"

I can't stop the hope seeping through my voice. I know she's not agreeing to a life with me just yet, but she's not forcing a pen into my hand either.

"Yeah." She nods with a shy smile.

I want to kiss her so badly it hurts, but I don't want to turn this moment into something sexual.

I've been so focused on the fact that her body still wants mine, that I've neglected to think too hard about what her mind wants.

Sex is the easy part.

It always has been with her and I.

It's all the other bullshit in between that I'm going to have to figure out.

I settle for kissing her forehead softly.

She sighs and rests her face against my chest.

"You showed me something yesterday, is it my turn today?" she asks after a long moment of silence.

"Whatever you want, princess. I'll go anywhere with you."

***

"I came here nearly every day," she tells me as she looks out at the horizon wistfully. "It was the only place that could keep me calm for a long period of time after you were gone."

I can see how it would.

There's something serene about the sound of the ocean waves crashing against the shore.

She pulls my hand as she comes to a stop and sits down in the dry, golden sand.

We've been walking along this beach for an hour, neither of us saying anything much at all.

No words have been needed.

I'm just enjoying being here with her. Walking along the sand, holding my wife's hand in silence is so far from the usual speed and pressure of my life, I don't really know how to process it.

You never relax in prison – if you do, that's when you'll find yourself in trouble.

You're always waiting, watching, preparing...

And ever since I got out, I've thrown myself onto my bike, into the business and now at Dylan.

It's been one high-speed ride after the other and taking this time to relax and unwind is something I didn't even realise I needed.

I need to breathe and let go.

I've got everything that's of any real significance to me right here next to me. She's safe and smiling.

There's nothing I need to think or worry about in this moment.

There's no immediate danger I need to plan for.

I just need to keep her smiling and everything else will sort itself out.

"It suits you out here," I tell her as I sink down to the ground next to her.

It's not exactly beach weather, and my ass is already fucking freezing, but I know I'd sit here in this cool sand with her all night if that's what she wanted.

She breathes in a deep breath, like she's just absorbing everything. "You think so?"

I nod. "Yeah, princess, I do."

She runs her hand through the sand and collects a handful before slowly letting it run back out between her fingers.

This is the most at peace I've seen her since she came crashing back into my office and into my life.

"Tell me what it was like when I was gone."

She glances at me from the corner of her eye before repeating the action with the handful of sand.

"It was hell," she replies simply.

I stare at her with a pained expression, but she doesn't look up at me to see it.

"I don't know how else to explain it. I went from having everything I ever wanted, to having next to nothing, all in the blink of an eye."

I feel like the biggest bastard in the world, hearing those words coming from her mouth.

She's so *good* – so innocent in this whole mess. And I made her life hell.

She went through hell because of *me* and it doesn't seem right that she's allowing me to be here next to her again.

"How'd you survive?" My voice sounds raw and strained.

She looks up at me now and shrugs. "Probably the same way you did... friends, distractions, anger... I smashed a few things."

Dylan's always had one hell of a temper on her, but there's not a violent bone in her body – she must have been so close to the edge to physically break something. I must have really pushed her to her limit this time.

"Sarah has been a godsend."

"She'd do anything for you, princess."

"I know." She smiles. "She even offered to hire someone to beat you up in prison – said she knew a guy."

I laugh. That sounds exactly like the Sarah I knew.

"I didn't get the delivery."

"I politely declined." She sighs.

"Tell me about what I've missed," I prompt her.

I don't miss that she freezes up for a fraction of a second before relaxing again.

She's drawing patterns in the sand now with a small stick. She makes a design and then wipes it away with a swipe of her hand and starts over again.

"There's three years' worth of stories, Andy."

"Then tell me," I whisper. "Tell me all of it... tell me everything I missed these past three years, Dylan. I want to hear every second of it... I want to know everything about it, about *you*." The intensity in my voice surprises me.

She looks up at me. "You already know I sold the house. I sent Jeff all of your stuff."

This isn't news to me – I know all this already.

I want to tell her to hurry up and tell me something new, but I bite my tongue.

Being an impatient prick isn't going to do me any favours.

"I got the apartment... changed jobs..."

"Why *did* you change jobs, princess?"

She shrugs. "I just felt like a fresh start."

I hear what she's not saying. She wanted to escape everything that reminded her of me.

Everyone in her old job knew me. There were photos of the two of us scattered all over her desk.

We'd had sex in her office. Repeatedly.

I can understand why she needed to leave.

"You like your new job?"

I reach for a strand of her long hair and play with it as I question her.

She smiles now – really genuinely smiles and I feel the knot in my gut ease a little bit.

I didn't fuck up her life entirely.

"I really love it. I never thought I'd like working for a paper, but it's the best. Like Stu probably told you, I haven't had more than a day off at a time since I started."

I chuckle. Stu said a lot of things – most of them sexual innuendos, but he did mention the huge amount of leave Dylan had owing and that she deserved a break.

"It's so much more diverse than the magazine ever was. I'm not just writing about meaningless gossip anymore. I get to meet real people and write about things that really matter. I never realised what I was missing out on."

She's got a fire in her belly about this – I can see it radiating from her.

"It sounds pretty fucking cool, princess."

She giggles. "It's *very* fucking cool."

As much as I love hearing about her job, I want more – I want to know the deep, meaningful shit.

"What else did I miss?"

She shrugs. "Not much. My parents still don't speak to me..."

I shake my head in disbelief. Dylan's parents stopped talking to her after she accepted my marriage proposal.

They said that two months of knowing one another wasn't enough to build a life on – that and the fact they didn't think a tattoo-covered, grease monkey was a good enough match for their daughter.

They weren't wrong – I've never been good enough for Dylan, but that didn't stop me from reaching out and taking her anyway, and it certainly didn't stop Dylan from coming with me.

I promised her it was a choice that I'd never make her regret, but I broke that promise.

They haven't spoken even a single word to her since the day she started wearing my ring on her finger, because despite their blackmail attempts and all common sense, Dylan still chose me.

I glance down at her hand – my ring isn't there. I'm not surprised, but it still stings.

"Your parents are idiots."

She huffs out a laugh in agreement. She's always said she wasn't bothered by their stance on our relationship – that their inability to accept me was on them and not on her, but I know it hurts her, she wouldn't be human if it didn't.

Especially now, when I've gone and essentially proved them right. They always said I was bad news for their daughter.

I bet they were right there waiting with their 'I told you so's' when I got put away.

"Do they know I got locked up?"

She nods. "Ohhh yeah. They weren't quiet about it either. First time I heard from them in years and it was only so they could gloat about being right... then they went straight back to pretending I didn't exist."

"Fuck, I'm sorry, Dylan."

She peeks up at me. "I know you are."

"You're not wearing your ring," I say in an attempt to distract her from her douche bag parents.

She glances down at her hand as though she needs to check for herself that it's not there.

"I couldn't look at it."

"Do you still have it?"

"Of course I still have it, Andy, I'm not the kinda girl to throw things off a bridge."

I chuckle. "Don't tell me you didn't consider it."

"Well I don't want to lie..." She smirks.

"I'm still wearing mine." I hold up my hand to her. I'm wearing a plain gold band – exactly the same as the one that used to adorn her finger. She never wanted a big fancy engagement ring, no matter how much I wanted to buy one for her – she wanted us to be equals.

"I know. I saw it the first day."

"You never said anything. I thought you would have told me to take it off."

Actually, I thought she would have yelled and screamed and pried it from my cold dead hand if she'd had to – but I keep that thought to myself – there's no need to give her any ideas.

"You wanna know something stupid?" she asks.

"Course I do."

"I was glad. I might have thought I was ready to move on from you, but the idea of *you* doing it – of you being with someone else made me sick to my stomach."

"That's not stupid, princess."

"It *is* stupid. I can't have it both ways."

An unwelcome thought creeps back into my mind at her statement.

I'd considered it was a possibility that she had dated while I was gone. In fact, I'd half expected her to have a live-in boyfriend by now – a woman like Dylan catches eyes everywhere she goes – but hearing her practically confirm it is something different.

"You've dated?" I ground out the words – they physically cause me pain, but I need to know.

She nods but doesn't look at me.

Rage surges through my veins to the point where I'm nearly shaking.

I know I need to get a grip on myself, blowing up at her now isn't going to fix anything. I can't even be mad at her. She was free to do whatever or whoever she liked.

I take a deep breath, and like the total sucker for punishment that I am, I ask her, "How many?"

"How many what?"

"Men, Dylan. How many men?"

"Ummm." She scribbles in the sand nervously. "Three. Well technically one was about ten men..."

She glances up at me and I must have fury written all over my face because she quickly explains.

"Speed dating. I went speed dating."

"Speed dating," I repeat, my voice strained.

"So that and two other men."

"Your neighbour?"

My jaw is tense as I wait for her answer.

"I told you I never said yes to him," she whispers.

I don't know why it makes me feel better, but it does. At least now I can't visualise the other men that have had their hands on my wife's body.

"Andy, I—"

"You don't need to explain. I get it," I interrupt her.

I kick at the sand with my foot in frustration.

I know it's my own fault. I left her. She didn't deserve to be alone while I was gone, but fuck if it doesn't cut me deep – right down to the core.

"No actually, I *do* need to explain," she snaps. "As far as I was concerned, we were over, Andy. *Done*. You weren't coming back to me. So yes, I went on a couple of dates. *Yes,* I let a guy buy me dinner. But I never slept with another man while you were gone. Even though you didn't deserve it, it just didn't feel right. I didn't want to be with someone that wasn't you."

"You didn't have sex with anyone else?" I say in disbelief.

The weight that has just been thrown off my shoulders nearly knocks me backwards.

I don't think I've ever felt relief like this.

I didn't deserve it – she's right about that, but fuck am I grateful for it nonetheless.

"No." She shakes her head. "I had two first dates, Jesus, Andy, what kind of girl do you think I am?"

I shoot her a look, and she blushes. "You had sex with me on our first date," I remind her.

"That doesn't count." She smacks my arm with a cheeky smile. "That was with *you*. You can't use our relationship as an example against me."

"Just pointing out that there are exceptions to all the rules, princess."

"*You're* the exception to all the rules," she mutters under her breath.

I grin at her. Fuck yes, I am.

"Within two hours of meeting you, Dylan, and I just fucking knew."

"Knew what?" She turns her body so she's leaning back against me, looking out at the sea.

"That I was going to make you my wife."

She giggles. "You did *not*."

"I did," I insist. "I text Jeff the minute you left and told him I'd just met the future Mrs. Woodman. You can even ask him."

I drag her over so she's sitting between my legs, her back against my front.

"Do you remember our wedding day?" she asks quietly.

"Of course I do."

I remember every single little thing about that day.

We might not have had a traditional wedding, but it was ours and that was all that mattered.

It was just us and our two best friends – back when they were more interested in screwing each other's brains out than they were in trying to kill one another.

Dylan didn't want anything big or flashy. She might be the kind of girl that wears makeup every day and keeps her nails and hair long and perfect, but she's not one for a big fuss. And she knew her family wouldn't have come either way.

We were engaged after only eight weeks of meeting and married six months after that.

Everyone said it wouldn't last, and they've been close to being right about that, but there's still hope for us, and I'm fucking clinging to it with both hands.

Her parents are idiots for losing Dylan over this – no matter who she was marrying, she's their daughter.

"It really was the best day."

"Best day of my life, fucking hands down."

She twists and looks up at me. "We had it all figured out..."

"We still do, princess, we just took a little detour, that's all."

CHAPTER EIGHTEEN

Dylan

It's already day five.

That's all I can think about when I open my eyes, the morning sun streaming in through the crack in the curtains.

Andy is still passed out next to me.

He's been here only five days, yet it feels like he never left.

I can't imagine ever being without him after this.

The man's a god damn genius for coming up with this seven-day plan – he's made this more than hard for me – that's for sure.

It was never going to be easy to decide to be without him, but now I know it's near impossible.

He's been so good to me these past twenty-four hours. He kissed me until I fell asleep in his arms and not once did he try and take things further.

He's got the self-control of a saint. I've never wanted him quite as badly as I do now, but I need to take things slow. I need to be one hundred percent sure about all things Andy before I take that leap, because I know – just like the first time – there's no coming back from crossing that line with him.

He sucks you in, mind, body and soul. Every last bit of you becomes his for the taking.

I know he's waiting for me to say the words – he promised we wouldn't have sex unless I gave him the go ahead. The fact

129

that he's stuck with his word, makes me only more inclined to believe him when he says he didn't do what he was accused of.

He's not just telling me that he's trustworthy, he's showing me.

My heart and my head are in a constant back and forth battle of what's right and what's wrong and the continuous uncertainty isn't something I can take much more of.

I need real answers.

I need *facts*.

Facts and information are a big part of my life – they're my job. They're what I do best.

I slip out of bed, being careful not to disturb Andy from his sleep.

He looks so peaceful and innocent when he's asleep that I have to resist the urge to run my fingers over his handsome face.

I glance down at his toned chest – there's absolutely nothing innocent about that body of his.

I grab my cell phone and sneak out of the room before I do something that'll result in me waking him up and begging him to undress me.

I pad out to the living area and snuggle myself up on the couch with a blanket.

I scroll through my phone until I find the contact I'm after.

It's late – we've slept in – so I know he'll be up and working already.

The phone rings a few times before I hear him answer, "Well hello there, how's my little love bird?"

I laugh. I can always count on Stu to brighten my day.

"I'm good," I reply.

"No denial, huh? *Interesting*. Not that I blame you, I saw him for myself, and mmm, mmm, mmm, honey, that man is *fine*."

"Seriously, Stu, do you think about anything other than sex?" I laugh.

"Not with men that look like him strolling around, that's for *damn* sure."

I shake my head in amusement.

"But seriously, how *are* you? We miss you around here. Just sort things out with him already so we can have you back."

"Well that's actually kind of why I called..."

"If you're telling me you're leaving to go and see the world or have a bunch of babies or something with lover boy, I swear to god I will hang up this phone, *right now*," he threatens dramatically.

"I'm not going anywhere," I promise with a roll of my eyes. "I called for a favour. I need you to do some digging into Andy's case."

"Did it, doing it, already on it," he answers quickly. I hear him snapping his fingers at each use of the word 'it'.

"I'm sorry, what?" I question in confusion.

His answer has thrown me – it's not what I expected him to say at all.

"That sexy man of yours asked me to."

"He did?"

"He *did*."

"Well this is news to me."

"Speaking of news, I have some."

"You do?" I asked, totally bewildered by this unexpected turn of events.

"Don't sound so surprised, it's insulting," he replies in a sassy tone.

I hold back a laugh.

"I have to go, but why don't the two of you come on in and say hi when you're ready. We can talk then."

"Um yeah... sure," I reply.

"Ciao!" he says before the line goes dead.

I shake my head in disbelief.

Andy appears in the doorway, scratching his head – wearing only a pair of basketball shorts again – but unlike last time, I'm more than happy with the situation.

"I woke up and you were gone," he complains with a yawn.

"I've just been talking to Stu."

He looks at me sheepishly. "Busted."

"He's got something he wants to show you."

"Yeah?"

"He told us to come in later."

"*Us*." He smirks. "I like the sound of that."

I shrug at him. "What's the point in hiding, the whole world knows we've got unfinished business, right?"

"They sure do, princess." He grins. "They sure do."

***

"I fucking *told you*, princess," Andy announces loudly.

If all the women in the office weren't already acutely aware of the man that walked in here with me, they would be now.

"Yeah." Stu smirks at me. "He fucking told you, *princess*."

I narrow my eyes at my husband's new number one supporter.

"Yeah, yeah, okay... who is he?"

"His name is Colin Albert Terry. My source tells me he's the man you're looking for and that he's picked up his operation and moved down the coast – new location, same old tricks."

"Asshole," Andy mutters. "I fucking knew it."

"Is this him?" Stu asks as he holds out a photo for Andy to look at.

"That's him," he growls after a brief glance.

I reach for his hand and take it in mine.

Stu watches the action with a knowing smile on his face.

"I told you, princess," he repeats in a whisper as his fingers tighten around mine.

"You did," I whisper back in guilty agreement.

I feel like the worst wife in the history of the universe.

This might not exactly be concrete evidence but it's enough for me to believe that Andy is telling me the truth. That he didn't steal that bike or any of those cars.

It's only confirming what I now realise I already knew. Deep down I think I believed him from the second the truth left his mouth, I just didn't want to accept it.

I doubt this information Stu has found would stand up in court – but it doesn't need to anyway, the time has already been served. Andy and I have already paid the price.

"I'm sorry," I choke out. "I'm so, so sorry, Andy."

He looks at me with tender eyes. "You have *nothing* to be sorry for."

He's wrong. I do.

He sweeps a strand of hair from my face and looks at me with so much love it almost hurts.

"You two are very sweet and all, but can we get back to the evidence please?" He taps the table impatiently.

"Hit me with it, Stu." Andy turns his focus from me to my work mate, and it's just as well. I couldn't take much more of his intense brown eyes without breaking down.

"I'd hit you with something alright." Stu winks.

I bite back a laugh. "And moving on..."

"Right, moving on." Stu nods with a cheeky grin. "I did some research into the case, and if you can prove that this Colin Terry fella is the one who is really to blame, you could get your conviction overturned."

Andy shrugs. "What's the point? I already did the time. I only looked into all of this for Dylan. She's the only thing I lost that I wanted back." He looks at me with such tenderness, my heart swells to twice its normal size.

Stu glances at me "*Girl*, did you hear that? Be *still* my beating heart." He clutches his chest dramatically and Andy laughs.

I shake my head in amusement. "Get on with it, Stu."

"Right, so... other than wiping the conviction from your record, you could be entitled to a sizeable payout for the time you served. You were wrongly convicted, and that kind of thing doesn't get taken lightly. You're innocent, Andy."

"But I'm not totally innocent though," Andy tells him in a pained voice. "*No*, I didn't steal those cars, but I knew something was up and I didn't say a word, it's like they *bought* my silence. I should have spoken up or turned them away, but instead I shut my mouth and jumped at the chance to make some extra money."

Extra money for *us*, I think to myself.

Every single cent that Andy bought home went into our home... building our life together.

He was making good money – I was too, and we were doing well for ourselves.

And then just like that, all the good things came to an end. Every little bit of positivity was sucked away.

It's like a punch to the gut every time I think about those months that followed him being taken from me.

I used to look at it as though he'd left me – but now I know the truth – he was *taken*.

That dodgy man, the law, the court system... they all took him from me.

I feel angry. So angry, and I know there's a chance I'm using this anger to mask my own guilt, but I don't care.

They took my husband from me when I needed him most.

He might not be perfect, but no one is – myself least of all.

There's still things he doesn't know – things I need to tell him. Things that are more important than overturned convictions or payouts, or who believed who.

I need to tell him everything.

He turns to look at me, and I notice that Stu is doing the same.

"Whaa— what?"

"What do you think, princess? Do you think I should let sleeping dogs lie or chase this?"

I look between my best work mate and the love of my life.

"Throw that asshole under the bus and take the bastards for all they're worth."

CHAPTER NINETEEN

Andy

"You still eat popcorn like a dinosaur." I chuckle as I watch her shovel another handful into her mouth.

She stops long enough to flip me the middle finger before continuing.

"It's cute, I like it."

She finishes her mouthful and takes a sip of her drink.

"You wanna know what's *not* cute?" she asks as she sits down the bowl and her glass.

I smirk at her. "I bet you're gonna tell me."

"You still snore like a freight train."

I toss a piece of popcorn in the air and catch it in my mouth. "I don't snore, princess," I tell her as I chew.

She makes a disbelieving snort noise before grabbing the remote and hitting pause on the movie we're watching and turning her body to face mine. "You're kidding, right?"

"Nope." I wink as I catch another piece.

"I could have killed you in your sleep last night and I would have been able to plead self-defence," she tells me, all sass and attitude.

"How do you figure that one?" I chuckle.

"It was assaulting my ears." She smirks. "So, self-defence."

I laugh at her and she lets out a little victorious giggle before going back to shovelling her precious popcorn into her mouth.

She turns back to the screen and hits play, settling in to watch again.

Her red hair is piled into a messy bun on the top of her head and she looks the picture of perfection clothed in a tight white tank top and grey sweatpants.

I've never seen anything as beautiful as her right now. From the freckles on her nose to the scar on her right foot – she's flawless in my eyes.

I'm the luckiest bastard in the history of the universe.

"God, I love you, Dylan."

Her hand freezes halfway to her mouth and she slowly turns to look at me.

"Don't look so shocked – you know I love you, princess."

"I haven't heard you say that in a really long time," she breathes.

"I loved you every single one of those hours we spent apart, Dylan, I loved you even when you hated me."

"I never hated you," she whispers.

I raise a brow at her.

"I didn't," she insists. "I *wanted* to hate you – god, I really did. But I couldn't... not completely. It's really hard to hate someone you love, Andy."

Her words aren't a surprise to me.

I know she loves me. I'm not some idiot that can't see what's in front of him. She's always loved me, and she always will – even if I were to walk out that door and never see her again, I know she'd love me until she died.

But contrary to what I told her, her loving me isn't the point of this week together. Her admitting that she loves me

– accepting that love and embracing it – *that's* what this is all about.

I don't even care if she admits it to me or not right now, as long as she admits it to herself then everything will be okay for us with time.

There's no way I'm going to let go of a woman like her without one hell of a fight.

"I know you love me, Dylan."

Her eyes trace over my face as her teeth graze her bottom lip.

She's thinking.

This is her fight or flight moment.

"You've loved me for nearly six years, princess." I shrug.

"I have," she whispers.

"I've loved you since the minute you smiled at me."

"I know." She smiles again – that same smile, and just like the first time, I'm totally fucking blindsided.

I'm hit with it all again – just how hard this must have been for her out here without me.

I would have gone crazy if she'd up and left me. I damn near went crazy as it was.

"I'm so fucking sorry," I choke out the words.

My emotions are threatening to overwhelm me right now, something that never happens to me.

Dylan has never seen me cry. She's seen me angry, but not often upset – and never enough to shed a tear.

She crawls towards me and climbs into my lap.

"Andy," she whispers. "I'm sorry too. I didn't believe you."

She's got tears in her eyes that are threatening to fall, and they only make me feel worse for all I've put her through.

She's got my face clasped in her hands as she looks at me with big, hurt eyes.

"I put that look in your eyes, Dylan, how can you even begin to forgive me?"

"It wasn't your fault," she tries to soothe me.

"I left myself open for it."

"It wasn't your fault," she repeats.

I wrap my arms around her waist and tug her even closer to me. I tuck my face into the crook of her neck and breathe her in.

"I'm the one who should be sorry," she whispers. "Not you."

I shake my head against her skin. "*No*."

"*Yes*," she argues. "What kind of wife am I? Walking away from you like that..."

"A smart one," I tell her as I pull back to look at her. "You saw the evidence, you know my past isn't exactly squeaky clean – I was caught on a stolen bike for fuck's sake... no one in their right mind would have believed my story over those facts."

"*I* should have believed you."

"And *I* should have never got myself – got *us* – in that situation."

We stare at each other for a long, long moment before she slowly and deliberately leans in to kiss me.

It's not a passion-fuelled haze like it so often is with Dylan – this is something different.

This feels like falling in love with her all over again.

Her lips are so soft and warm and she's inviting me in.

I tug her closer again until there's no space left between us, so we're one again.

I thought about this moment so often while I was locked up, but my imagination didn't do it anywhere near justice.

The smell of her, the feel of her body and mouth against mine is too good to be conjured up in the mind.

She's too good.

Her lips break away from mine and she sucks in a deep breath.

"I love you, Drew," she whispers on her exhale. "I'm *so* in love with you."

It's so quiet, but I hear her words.

"I've been waiting for you to catch on," I reply huskily.

She looks like she has something more she wants to say, but I don't push it – she's already said the most important thing. We can work through anything else later.

She runs one of her hands through my hair, pushing it away from my eyes.

"I'm saying the words, Drew."

"I heard them, princess."

I fucking heard them all the way down to my toes.

"*No*." She shakes her head. "I'm saying *the words*."

She bites down on her lip nervously and that's when I hear what she's really saying.

She wants me – *all* of me.

She's giving me the green light.

"Are you sure?" I manage to choke out.

I want to be inside her more than I've ever wanted anything, but I have to know she's one hundred percent ready for this.

She nods her head. "I'm sure."

That's good enough confirmation for me.

I push to my feet in one swift movement – taking her with me as I go.

She gasps and wraps her legs around my waist to hold on tight.

I carry her to the bedroom, my brown eyes never leaving her green ones.

I'm so wound up I can barely think straight, but I know enough to figure out I have to take this slow.

There will be plenty of time for hard and fast – we've got the rest of our lives.

Right now is the time for savouring and remembering. I have to learn her body all over again.

I sit down on the edge of the bed and kiss the tip of her nose. "I love you," I tell her, my voice raw and vulnerable.

"I love *you*," she whispers back.

I kiss down her cheek, neck and along her collarbone.

"How'd I get so lucky?" I murmur against her skin.

She moans as I lightly trail my fingers up her sides, lifting her top as I go.

She lets go of my neck as I pull it over her head.

I take my time looking at her, recommitting every curve of her body to memory.

"You're so beautiful, princess."

A blush stains her cheeks as she reaches for the hem of my t-shirt.

"Lift up," she instructs softly.

"I knew you'd decide shirts were a bad idea eventually."

She tugs the t-shirt over my head and grins at me. "I've had the self-control of a saint," she mutters.

Her hands roam over my chest, her fingers following the patterns of my tattoos before moving to the hard grooves of my abdomen.

She's barely touched me yet and I'm already so wired. She's lighting me on fire with every stroke of her fingers.

I hoist her up and turn her so her back lands on the bed with a soft thud.

I reach for the waistband of her sweatpants and tug them down her golden legs.

The woman of my dreams is right here, wearing nothing but a white lace bra and a pair of black, skimpy underwear.

I seriously can't believe my luck. All the bad shit I've done in my life, but yet I still have *her*.

There must be some poor prick out there somewhere with the worst luck in the world, because I somehow managed to get a double share.

She giggles and it's only then that I realise I'm just hovering over her on my knees, staring.

"Do you need another photo?" she asks coyly.

"I don't need a photo," I growl. "I've got the real thing right here."

"Come and get me then."

I don't need to be told twice.

I lower my body to hers and kiss her until I'm lightheaded.

"*Drew*," she moans and it's just like in every one of my fantasies.

"Yeah, princess?" I ask in between placing kisses to her neck.

"Don't stop."

I chuckle. I've got absolutely no intention of stopping.

I pull back so I'm on my knees again, looking down at the perfection that is my wife.

I hook my thumbs into her underwear and drag them slowly down her legs.

She's writhing beneath me as I look down at her.

That's when I notice the mark that I've never seen before.

It's only faint, but there's no way I would possibly miss a single thing about this woman.

I lower myself down to get a closer look.

It's a tattoo, but instead of the usual black ink, this is done in white. It's on her left side, in a spot that would normally be hidden beneath her underwear.

It simply reads '*Nina*'.

"Princess?" I question.

"Mmm?" she replies as her hands comb lazily through my hair.

"Who is *Nina*?"

She freezes, her hands drop from my head and her whole body stiffens.

I look away from the word etched into her skin and glance at her face.

She's terrified and I have no idea what's wrong.

A pained sob rips out of her mouth and she pulls her body from underneath mine and scoots up the bed, clutching her knees to her chest as she goes.

I grab the throw blanket off the end of the bed and drape it over her – she's physically shaking, and I've never been more afraid in my whole life.

I'm too scared to even touch her right now.

"Dylan?" I whisper when she doesn't answer. "Who's Nina?"

She stares at me with so much pain, my life feels like it's going to end.

Tears well in her eyes as she whispers her answer, "She was our daughter."

I don't know what I expected her to say, but I never would have guessed that in a million years.

Those four words send my whole universe into a tailspin.

"Our... our *daughter*?" I stutter as another realisation hits me. "*Was*? Princess, what do you mean *was*?"

I can feel the weight of the world pushing down on my shoulders and I physically sag onto the bed to try and escape it.

"The day you got arrested, I found out I was pregnant," she whispers, and I can hear the pain in her voice.

"I was waiting for you to get home so I could surprise you and we could celebrate... you never came."

I feel tears welling in my own eyes now and I know that they're going to fall this time.

This is the thing that's going to finally break me.

"So that's when I came down to the garage to find you. I was so excited."

I remember the moment like it was yesterday. I can still picture the look of joy in her eyes until it all came crumbling down.

"I was about eight weeks," she carries on, her voice still a whisper.

"And I left you," I choke out the words.

I know now that this is why she didn't come to see me – why she didn't call.

I didn't just leave her – I left *them*.

I left my wife, pregnant and alone.

I left her with the future of bringing up a baby on her own when I should have been there with her.

"I know I should have told you, but I didn't know how."

I shake my head – I don't want her shouldering any of the blame on this one. This is all on me.

"What happened to her?" I whisper, already knowing that the answer is going to crush me.

"I was driving to the prison – to tell you I was pregnant."

Ice runs cold in my veins as I wait for the next part.

"I wasn't paying enough attention." Her voice cracks as our eyes meet.

Tears are silently running down her face and it breaks my heart.

"There was a crash. I wound up hitting the back of the car in front of me. It wasn't anything major, but the driver airbag deployed..."

I nod my head in acceptance of what I already know happened.

"I lost the baby. I was twenty-three weeks along."

My chest constricts as I gasp for air. I can feel the tears overflowing from my eyes as my vision blurs.

She lost our baby because of *me*.

Because I wasn't there.

"I didn't protect her." She sobs.

I can't speak. I want to tell her that it's not her fault – that's it's yet another thing that's on my conscience, but I can't.

I should have been there to protect both of my girls, but I wasn't.

It's all I can think about as I stand up off the bed on shaky legs.

I know this is going to haunt me for the rest of my days.

I pick up my shirt off the floor and walk out the door. I don't know where I'm going but I do know I can't be here right now. I can't watch her heart breaking all over again because of me.

I need air.

I spent three years in a box and right now I need to breathe.

I almost run out to the living room and I'm about to swing open the door when the stack of papers on the table catches my eye.

I know now why she needed me to sign – why she didn't want to call herself my wife for a minute longer.

I can't blame her for that. She deserves so much more than a man like me.

I grab the pen and scrawl my signature on the dotted lines.

She wanted a clean break and like the asshole I am, I didn't give it to her.

I forced my way back into her life and her heart and now she's broken all over again because of it.

"I'm so sorry, Dylan, I love you," I whisper as I slip out the door.

CHAPTER TWENTY

Dylan

He cried.

I've never, ever seen him lose control of his emotions like that.

His eyes glistened on our wedding day, but he didn't allow a single tear to escape and even that reaction had overwhelmed me.

But that was nothing compared to what I just saw.

He wasn't just heartbroken when I told him; it was as though some type of bomb had detonated in his chest, totally and utterly destroying him from the inside out.

I know how he feels – losing our daughter did the same thing to me.

I drag myself up from the spot I'm still sitting in on my bed.

I'm virtually naked and I can still feel the heat on my skin from where he touched me.

My head was so full of him, I never even thought about my tattoo until it was too late.

He needed to know – I know I had to tell him, but it shouldn't have been like that.

He was right all along – we did have unfinished business, but it's over now. Every secret between us has been hung out to dry and just like I thought it would be – the fallout was too much.

The day we got married, I promised him that we could withstand any storm, but I was wrong. I was only twenty years old, and I might have been naive about a lot of things, but I was sure about him. I loved him something fierce – I still do.

This is a storm we couldn't weather, and as much as it pains me that this is how it's going to end, I'm relieved that he finally knows.

I've struggled a lot these past couple of years, not only with the grief, but with the guilt too.

I reach for my sweatpants and slide them back up my legs. My top follows next.

The whole house feels like it's echoing with emptiness around me as I walk slowly into the living room.

He's really gone.

He might be out there free in the world, and not locked behind bars, but this time the separation feels a lot more permanent.

Everything feels strange and weightless. It's all just empty.

I feel lost. So I do the only thing I can think of. I call my best friend.

I know one of these days, Sarah is going to stop taking my calls; more often than not it's bad news I'm delivering, but I hope like hell that today isn't that day, because I need her right now.

Maybe more than I ever have.

"Hey, girl," she answers cheerily.

"He's gone, Sare," I blurt out.

"What do you mean, he's gone?"

"He's *gone*." I can feel my bottom lip wobbling and I know I'm going to have a meltdown before too much longer. "I told him about Nina and he left."

"Oh, Dylan," she breathes. "I'm so sorry."

"Me too," I whimper.

"He didn't take it well?" she asks softly.

"He was in shock. It's all my fault, Sare, I did this to him."

"*None* of this is your fault."

"Isn't it? If I'd just told him about the baby in the first place I wouldn't have been there that day – Nina might still be alive."

"You don't know that, D. You didn't do anything wrong."

"He's gone." I sob, the words on repeat in my head.

"Did he say where he was going?"

I shake my head even though she can't see it. "He just walked out."

"He might come back," she tries to soothe me. "Maybe he just needs some time to process it."

She's wrong. He's gone for good.

He blames me, and he's gone.

"He signed the papers," I choke out as I run my fingers over the scrawl of his signature.

"Oh, Dylan..." She sighs. "Are you at home? I'll come over."

"No," I reply quickly. "I'm okay, I just need to be by myself for a little bit."

I need some time to be alone so I can break down and let it all out.

"I really don't think that's the best idea, D."

"I'm okay," I promise her. "I've been through all this before, remember?"

"That's what I'm afraid of."

"I'll be fine, I'll call you in the morning, okay?"

"You call me at *any* hour if you need me, got it?"

"I got it. Thanks, Sare... I love you."

"I love you too, you'll be okay, D, I promise."

***

I sit and stare at the door for what feels like hours and hours, when in reality I know only about forty minutes has passed since I sat down.

This is what my life will be like now.

Every minute without him will feel like an eternity.

I'll forever be waiting and wishing for him to come back to me.

The notion haunts me as I feel my lids getting heavy – my exhausted mind and body are submitting to sleep.

"*Drew*," I hear myself say as I drift off.

CHAPTER TWENTY-ONE

Andy

I burst into the garage like a man who's running from the cops.

I'm sweating bullets and my heart is racing.

I don't even remember getting on my bike and driving over here, yet here I am.

It's dark out – I don't know even what time it might be. In my haste to leave I forgot to take my cell phone with me.

I'm not sure why I came here of all places, but I guess when I consider the options, I don't actually have anywhere else to go.

I expected the garage to be empty, but given the current dose of karma I've received, there's no such luck.

"Jesus, Wood, what the fuck happened to you?"

"I... I... I..." I stutter, giving him nothing to go on.

I wasn't prepared to be confronted. I'm not ready to share the imploding of my life.

Jeff jogs over to me and throws his arm over my shoulder and steers me towards a chair. He pushes down on me until I'm sitting in it.

It's like I've forgotten how to talk and walk. I can't do anything right now.

"Wood? What the fuck is wrong with you? You gotta talk to me, man."

"Dylan," I blurt out.

The sound of her name causes me to double over, my head falling into my hands.

"Jesus, is Dylan okay?"

I stutter something incoherent.

"I'm calling her," Jeff announces.

I can hear the cell phone ringing out as he waits for her to pick up.

She won't.

I know she won't.

She must hate me – she'd have to... and Jeff's my best friend, so she probably hates him too – guilty by association and all that shit.

"Fuck," he mutters as his call goes unanswered.

"Andy, is Dylan okay?" he demands as he crouches down in front of me.

"She... She... I..."

"Fuck," he mutters again as he gets to his feet.

I don't know who he's ringing this time, but I hear him hiss, "pick up the phone you little she-devil."

"Sarah, thank fuck, don't hang up okay? It's important, just listen," he demands.

He called *Sarah*. Jeff swore he was never talking to that woman ever again – so he must be really fucking worried if he's calling her now.

"It's about Andy."

"No, he's here. He's a wreck."

There's silence as he listens.

"She's okay?" I hear him release a relieved breath. "Thank fuck."

I don't know what Sarah's saying, but I know it won't be anything good.

I left Dylan half naked, crying and afraid.

I'm the biggest bastard on the face of the earth.

"Oh Jesus," he chokes out, his voice pained. "Yeah okay, I've got him." Silence. "Yeah I got it. Okay. Thanks."

More silence.

"Wood?" he asks cautiously as he crouches down in front of me again.

I nod but don't look up.

"Sarah told me about the baby, I'm so fucking sorry, man."

That does it.

The last of the control I had hold of snaps and I break down in a wave of gut-wrenching tears.

Jeff doesn't say anything. He just hugs me through what might be the most vulnerable moment of my life.

***

"She named her Nina," I tell Jeff as I spoon sugar into the coffee he's just made me.

My initial, paralysing shock seems to have worn off, and while I still feel numb, I've figured out how to speak again at least.

"That's a sweet name."

I take a sip of the hot liquid and feel it burn all the way down to my stomach. I welcome it. The burst of pain is the least I deserve after everything I've put Dylan through.

"She had to deal with it on her own, it's no fucking wonder she wanted a divorce."

"It's not your fault you weren't there, Wood. Don't you try and take the blame for this."

"Then whose fault is it?" I snap at him. "I had a daughter I didn't even know about and now she's gone."

"It's no one's fault. There's no one to blame for this, Andy, you didn't make this happen."

"She blames me," I choke out. "And she's right."

"Did she say that?"

"She didn't have to."

"Why don't you tell me what went down between you two?" he prompts. "Because if there's one thing I know about you, Wood, it's that you take the blame for shit when you don't have to – you always have."

He's fucking wrong, but he won't give in and let me wallow in peace until he's heard it all – start to finish.

So I tell him.

He's been quiet for a few minutes now, just absorbing the information I've given him.

"So, let me get this straight," he finally says. "She told you that she loves you and she was going to let you back... you know... *in*."

He gestures with his hands, making a circle with one hand and sticking his finger in on the other hand.

"What are you? Five? We were about to have sex, Stonesie. Fuck, and you wonder why you haven't got yourself a woman."

He chuckles and grins at me like the immature fucker he is. "Right, so she loves you and she's going to let you bone her, right?"

"For lack of a better explanation, yeah."

"Then you're a fucking *idiot*." He shakes his head at me in disbelief.

"*I'm* the idiot? That's rich coming from you."

"I'm not the one who just left behind a woman who loves me."

"She can't possibly love me after this, man."

"And that's where you're a god damn halfwit. You think she couldn't possibly want you because of what happened with the baby, right?"

I nod.

"This isn't new information to *her*, you moron, it's only new to you."

I stare at him in confusion.

He shakes his head like I'm a small child he can't be bothered dealing with.

"Jesus, and people say you're the smart one," he scoffs. "When she told you she loved you and she asked you to make love to her, she did all that, knowing *everything*... she knew that she lost the baby, and that you weren't there to support her through it. She knew it all and she wanted you despite it."

The big dumb bastard is right.

I just ran out on the love of my life for the second time, and all because I thought I knew something that I didn't.

"She doesn't blame me," I think aloud.

"Based on what you've just told me, man, I'd say she blames herself."

Guilt hits me like a smack in the face as I acknowledge the truth in his words.

That would be classic Dylan. She's so damn hard on herself.

She blames herself and I left her. I didn't say a word. So now she probably thinks I blame her too.

Christ, I *am* a fucking idiot.

"I gotta get back there."

"Smartest thing you've said all night," he drawls as I run from the room, snagging my keys off the table as I go.

"Give Dylan a hug for me," he yells after me.

I stop in my tracks and jog back into the break room toward my best mate.

I pull him in for a hug and clap him on the back. "Thanks, Jeff. I appreciate it. I don't know what I'd do without you."

"I shudder to think," he jokes. "And you're welcome, man, go get the girl."

I chuckle as I head off to beg for forgiveness for the second time this week.

CHAPTER TWENTY-TWO

Dylan

I wake to the brightness around me hurting my eyes.

It shouldn't be this bright in here.

I blink drowsily as I look around. I'm in the living room. I must have fallen asleep out here last night.

That's when it all hits me again.

He's gone.

I rub at my eyes and try to keep the tears at bay.

I've cried enough. Crying gets me nowhere. I really should have learnt that by now.

I sit up and open my eyes and my heart leaps in my chest at the sight in front of me - the gorgeous man sitting in the chair to my left.

"Good morning, princess," he says.

"You're here," I blurt.

"I've been here all night. I didn't want to wake you."

He looks totally shattered, like he's just survived twelve rounds of boxing.

"You're here," I repeat.

"I'm here, princess."

"*Why*?" I ask.

"Because you're here."

My head is screaming at me not to get my hopes up as we stare cautiously at one another.

"I'm so sorry, Andy." I say the words before I lose my cool and break down again. He needs to know how sorry I am – even if it's too late for us – I still need him to know.

"I'm so fucking sorry," he says at the same time.

"I should have told you," I whisper.

"I shouldn't have left you."

"I should have believed you."

"I shouldn't have given you a reason not to," he argues.

I groan in frustration. This is where putting two ridiculously stubborn people in the same room, let alone a relationship, is difficult.

Neither one of us wants to back down – even when we're both trying to take the blame rather than avoid it.

This is going to go around and around in circles... me blaming me and him blaming him.

It's too late now for should have or could have.

What's done is done.

It's too late for a lot of things – mainly for our little girl, but maybe it's not too late to fix things between us... I hope more than anything that we still have a shot at this, but I wouldn't blame him if he wanted to walk away for good.

"I killed our baby, Andy." I sob as my emotions and my guilt pour out of me.

He's on his feet in a flash and holding me before I even know what's happening.

"Princess, no," he soothes as I sob. "It was an accident. You didn't do anything wrong."

"I should have been able to stop in time."

"You did *nothing* wrong," he tells me over and over as he holds me in his arms.

"I should have been there for you. I should have been the one driving you around... you shouldn't have been coming to see me in prison. It's not your fault."

He holds me tight, rocking me gently side to side, trying to soothe me.

"I think about it, you know?"

"About what, princess?"

"About what it would have been like if I didn't get involved in that accident... if I'd made it to see you. I think about how your face would have looked – I think about how happy you would have been to hear you were going to be a father."

"Some father I would have been," he growls. "No child should have to visit their dad behind bars."

I don't have anything to say to that, because I know he's right. It's not something that I can imagine anyone wishing for.

Andy would have been a great father, he *will* be a great father when that time comes for him. But raising a baby without him isn't the life I wanted for myself or for my child.

"You'll be an amazing dad one day, Andy," I whisper.

"I hope so," he replies gruffly. "But the only way I'm doing that, is with you, Dylan."

My heart speeds up in my chest.

"So you still want to do this with me?" I ask timidly. It's a simple question, but one that carries the weight of the world to me.

"What, 'this' as in *marriage*?" he replies with a cheeky smirk.

I nod.

He cups my jaw in his big, rough hand and stokes his thumb over my lip.

"Fuck, yes I do, princess, I'm sure as hell not doing it without you anymore."

"You promise?" I whisper.

"I promise. Forever." His voice is thick and gravelly, and I know he means it.

He won't leave me ever again.

Our life might have been totally turned on its head, but nothing has ever felt as right to me as Andy does. I know I have to trust my gut on this one.

"And you want to have kids one day?"

"I want to have a whole heap of them."

I hope one day we'll be that lucky. I think we deserve the chance to have a family.

"Are you okay, Dylan? There's no damage to you... you know, from losing her?"

I shake my head. "Not physically. Everything still works like it should. The only damage is in my heart."

He rubs slow circles on my back as he looks into my eyes.

"I bet she would have been beautiful," he says, and it makes me love him just a little bit more.

"She was."

"I'm so sorry, Dylan," he says again.

I shake my head. "Right here and now, can we agree that there's nothing to be sorry for anymore – not from either of us?"

"But I—"

"No buts," I tell him. "I'll forgive myself if you forgive yourself."

"I don't need to forgive myself, princess, I need *you* to forgive *me*."

"All is forgiven," I say simply.

"You can't just let this all go."

"I already have," I tell him. "Why? Do you not forgive me?"

"There's nothing to forgive."

"Ditto," I reply simply.

He searches my face for any sign that I'm not being totally honest with him, but he'll find none, I know that already.

I'm all in. *Again.*

I look at him, my handsome husband, and sigh.

This is the sight I'm going to get to wake up to every single day, and I couldn't think of a better view. I did three whole years without seeing it, and I'm not willing to part with it another day.

"I love you, Drew, but I don't want you to be sorry anymore."

He nods his head, like maybe he's finally considering accepting that it's time for us to move on.

"There's just one more thing I need to do."

He untangles himself from around me and strides over to the table.

He picks up the divorce papers and rips them in half and then in half again and again.

I laugh as he totally destroys the sheets of paper.

"Feel better now?"

"Almost," he says as he balls up a scrap of paper and tosses it in his mouth.

"Did you just swallow that?" I ask in disbelief.

"You bet your ass I did." He smirks. "Now next time you get pissed off with me you can't dig all these bits out and stick them back together."

"Touché." I giggle.

"Smart, right?" He grins at me wolfishly.

"Knew I married you for a reason." I wink at him.

CHAPTER TWENTY-THREE

Andy

She strolls back into the room, and I groan in appreciation of the view in front of me.

"I don't know what I'm more excited about, that ass or my ring being back on your finger," I drawl.

There's really no competition – as fine as her ass might be, that ring has my head and my heart so full and satisfied, it's almost messed up.

She giggles and shakes her butt at me playfully.

I'm physically exhausted, she is too, but it's not going to stop me from looking – even if I'm too tired to do anything about it.

We've spent *all day* in bed and I don't know about Dylan, but without some type of special pill, three times in one day is my fucking limit.

I'm maxed out.

It's dark out now and I glance at the digital clock next to her side of the bed as she slides back in next to me.

She snuggles against me and makes a purr of appreciation at the warmth.

"It's after midnight, princess."

"Mmmm?"

"It's day seven," I say.

She tilts her head back so she can look up at me. "Huh... so it is."

I brush a strand of hair from her forehead. "What's the verdict?"

She smiles at me and pretends to ponder it for a moment. "I've got what I wanted, maybe I might send you packing now after all."

"Is that how it's gonna be?"

I tickle her ribs and she laughs and squirms.

"I'm joking!" she cries. "I swear I was joking."

"What was that, princess?" I question as I carry on tickling her. "You were implying you were only after me for my dick? Is that right?"

She rolls away from me as she laughs, and I drag her back towards me.

She looks up at me and bites down on her bottom lip. "I think I'll keep you," she whispers.

"You're not just after me for my penis powers?"

She sighs and grins. "They are some *good* powers."

I grin smugly.

"But even without them, I still think you might be worth keeping..." She blushes. "And besides, I can't get rid of you, you ripped up the papers, and ate half of it like some kind of deranged animal, remember?"

"Damn right I did."

I lean in and kiss her on the forehead in a gesture much softer and sweeter than what just went down in this bed a short time ago.

"I love you, Dylan."

She smiles at me like the words are music to her ears. "I love you too, Drew."

"I'm never going to leave you again. I won't fuck this up – not twice," I promise her.

She runs a finger down the side of my face. "I know you won't."

I kiss her forehead and close my eyes. "Get some sleep, princess, we've got shit to do tomorrow."

"We do?" she replies sleepily.

"Fuck, yes we do."

***

"C'mon, princess, the lawyer is waiting for us."

She stops in her tracks and sits her hands on her hips. "Have you ever tried walking in heels this high?"

I give her a 'what the fuck do you think' look, but being the stubborn ass that she is, she just stands there, waiting for an actual answer to her ridiculous question.

"Well?" she prompts with a brow arched.

"I can't say I have," I drawl.

"Well then, until you have, don't you fucking rush me, Andy, I'm not opposed to taking one of these off and throwing it at you."

The corner of my mouth twitches with amusement.

She's still so feisty. I've gotten used to being around men who don't give lip and attitude, but this isn't some dude, this is my wife – and she's full of fire. I just have to hope I remember how to avoid getting burnt.

"I'm sorry, princess, how about I take a pair for a spin later, so I know what you're up against?"

She tries her hardest to hold back a grin but fails miserably.

She strolls over, no faster than she was before and links her arm with mine. "As funny as that would be to watch, you keep those huge trotters away from my shoes, you got it?"

I chuckle as I hold the door open for her to go in ahead of me.

We're here to meet Tim, my defence lawyer.

I'm armed with every scrap of evidence that Stu was able to find for us and for the first time since all this bullshit went down, I actually feel a glimmer of hope.

Dylan glances around the space suspiciously. "I think we should have got you a new lawyer," she whispers.

"Tim's a good lawyer, Dylan."

"Really?" she hisses at me. "If he's such a great fucking lawyer, then why'd you end up in prison for three years?"

I chuckle as I lead her down the hall to his office. "I didn't give him a lot to work with."

"It didn't take Stu long to figure it all out, what were the cops and this so-called lawyer doing the entire time? Sitting around with their thumbs up their asses?"

"He's a pretty serious guy, princess, you might have to tone it down a bit."

She gives me a look that makes it clear she doesn't give a flying fuck about my warning.

"You're going to get me in trouble here, aren't you?"

She smirks at me as I knock on the door. "Probably."

Seeing my woman going into bat for me is one hell of a turn on – it just makes me realise how much I missed out on by not having her on my side in the beginning of this whole mess.

If I'd been more open and honest with my wife, maybe she would have believed me and stuck by me. And if I'd been less of a dodgy bastard in my work practices, then maybe I wouldn't have found myself in this fucking position in the first place.

It's been one hell of a learning curve – that's for damn sure. I might not be the sharpest tool in the shed, but I won't be making these mistakes twice.

I hear Tim call out for us to come in and I open the door, ushering Dylan in ahead of me.

"Tim, this is my wife, Dylan. Dylan, my lawyer, Tim."

"It's good to finally meet you, Dylan." He holds out his hand and Dylan warily reaches out to shake it without replying.

"We've got new info for you," I announce as Tim gestures for us both to sit down on the opposite side of the table.

I don't bother with pleasantries, I haven't got time for fucking around anymore – I've got a life to live now and I want to get on with it.

"You mentioned on the phone." He holds his hand out for the folder I've carried in with me.

I pass it over to him and wait somewhat nervously as he takes his time flicking through each page of the findings.

"Where did you get this?" he questions without looking up.

"I work for a newspaper," Dylan answers before I can. "My work colleague is the best investigative journalist in the business – he found that out."

"In less than a day," she adds in a mutter.

I smirk at her sassy comment.

Tim stops reading and glances up at her. He heard it too.

"This is impressive."

She looks back at him with a 'no shit' expression.

"You think it'll be any use?" I ask him before Dylan can start a fight.

"I'll have to get in touch with the arresting officer and the detective on your case, but if this information checks out, I'll be pushing to have your conviction ruled as wrongful and your stint in prison as wrongful imprisonment too."

"What happens if we do that and win?"

He glances at the information in front of him again. "I know I shouldn't say this – I don't like to make promises, but I've got no doubt that we'll win if these leads check out. If you want to go ahead and fight it that is?"

My heart speeds up. "And then?"

"Then your conviction will be removed from your record, and you should be awarded compensation."

"How much?" I growl.

I might have left myself in a vulnerable position by working on those cars, but I didn't deserve prison time and I'm willing to milk all I can get out of this if it goes my way.

He scrawls a figure down on a scrap of paper and slides it across the table to me.

Holy shit.

"*That* much?" Dylan gapes at Tim as she looks at the number over my shoulder.

"That's right."

"Can we throw him back in for a bit longer?" she quips.

I shake my head in amusement. "That's charming, princess, really charming."

She grins at me. "I'm kidding... kind of."

Tim actually cracks a smile at my wife.

I chuckle and hold my hand out for Tim to shake. "Do it."

CHAPTER TWENTY-FOUR

Dylan

"Where to now?" I ask him as I sit in the front seat of the classic Corvette he surprised me with this morning. It's the same one I admired in his garage only a week ago.

He looks so incredibly sexy sitting behind the wheel of this car.

It feels like this thing between us has been going on for an eternity already – I'm so comfortable with him again, but in reality, it's only been seven days.

He was right. He only needed a week.

"We're going to see Sarah," he replies, surprising me.

"Sarah? *Why*?"

He smirks at me as he weaves through traffic. "You'll see when we get there."

I try the entire trip to convince him to tell me what it is that he needs my best friend for, but he won't give the answer up.

I don't know how he knows where Sarah's new place is, but before I know it, we're parked outside.

I narrow my eyes at him and cross my arms over my chest as I watch him climb out of the car and round the hood.

He opens my door and chuckles at my expression.

"What?"

I raise my brow at him and shoot him a 'you know what' look.

He laughs again. "Stu," he offers with a shrug by way of explanation.

"He's such a little traitor," I grumble as I take his offered hand and let him guide me out of my seat.

Andy grins at me and pulls me against his firm chest. "We're on the same side now, princess."

"I know we are." I sigh and give in with a smile. "But I'm still going to argue with you."

"It wouldn't be any fun if you didn't." He smirks "Now hold my hand, your friend scares me."

I don't have a clue what we're doing here, but if I know Andy, it'll be something totally unnecessary.

He tugs me up the front steps and knocks on the door.

He shuffles from foot to foot nervously – I don't actually think he was joking when he said that Sarah scares him.

"Stop twitching," I tell him with a shit-eating grin. "She's like a wild animal, she'll smell your fear a mile away."

He's about to reply something smart when the door swings open and the retort is lost.

"Oh hey..." Sarah looks between the two of us in confusion. "What are you guys doing here?"

She looks back at me in confusion and I shrug.

I've got no more idea about what we're doing here than she does.

"*I* wanted to talk to you," Andy answers.

Sarah looks at him in surprise. "Alright then, Woodman, do you wanna come in?"

He shakes his head. "This won't take long – we have somewhere else to be."

I don't know where the hell else we're going, but apparently the excursions aren't done for the day.

We've been back together only one day officially, and he's already driving me crazy, but I'd be lying if I said I wasn't loving every second of it. The unknown is exciting.

I've always been content to sit back and let Andy take the wheel. I just hold on for the ride.

"Well you better get talking then," she prompts.

He takes a deep breath and I watch with interest.

"I wanted to say sorry to you, Sarah. I put Dylan through hell and you were the one that had to pick up the pieces. It can't have been easy for you to watch her go through that."

I can tell Sarah is surprised, maybe even shocked, but she does a good job of covering it.

"It wasn't the best time," she acknowledges after a beat.

"And I also wanted to thank you," Andy says.

She tilts her head to the side and eyes him curiously. "For what?"

"For taking care of her when she lost the baby. You can't possibly imagine how much I wish that it hadn't happened, or that I could have been there for her, but I wasn't. *You were.* I don't know how I can ever repay you for taking care of her – I know it wasn't for my benefit, but she's my whole life, so thank you." His voice cracks with emotion and I squeeze his hand tighter.

I can feel tears welling in my eyes.

This is so unexpected, I don't know how to deal with it.

Andy might have shown me that sensitive side of him a bit more lately, but he never, *ever* shows it to anyone else.

Sarah is being given a rare glimpse into the real Andy, and I hope she realises how much of a big deal this is.

Sarah looks like she might be going to cry too. She glances between Andy and I several times before speaking.

"I'm glad you're back, Andy," she tells him quietly. "She's never as happy as she is when she's with you."

She's right. He drives me insane, but it's the kind of insane I crave. I really do love this man like crazy.

"She's my princess," he answers with a shrug.

Sarah nods her head. "And even though it doesn't really matter, I accept your apology and I forgive you."

I look up at Andy and he's got one hell of a smile on his face. Sarah might not think it matters, but I can tell it matters a whole hell of a lot to my husband.

"Thank you," he says, his voice sounding like gravel. "You're her best friend and I hate to think where we'd be without you."

I shudder at the thought too. I wouldn't have got through any of this without the woman in front of me.

"Then *don't* think about it," she replies with a grin. "You mechanics aren't all that sharp, are you?" she teases.

Andy chuckles and just like that, it's back to the way it was before he left.

"You really don't wanna come in?" She gestures with her thumb over her shoulder.

Andy glances at his watch. "Next time? We've already gotta hustle."

"Come for dinner next week."

"Sounds good," Andy says.

I watch the interaction before me with utter bewilderment.

This is the same man who I've wanted to hate for three years, and the same woman who was right there encouraging me to give him the flick.

Now they're back to being best friends like nothing ever happened.

I wave over my shoulder at her as I'm dragged back down to the car by my husband who's muttering about being late and which way will have less traffic.

I pause outside the car and just take a moment to really look at him, even though I know it's bound to piss him off that I'm mucking around.

"Princess?" he questions.

I press up to my tiptoes and kiss his lips. "Thank you," I breathe as we break apart.

He brushes a strand of hair from my face. "You're welcome." He presses his lips to mine once more. "Now get in the car already, we're gonna be late."

***

I watch nervously as the tattoo artist grabs a clean paper towel and squirts some type of liquid onto it before wiping down Andy's skin.

The buzzing of the tattoo gun has brought back a lot of memories for me, it was only a few months after my miscarriage that I came to a place just like this one and asked for the one single word to be etched into my skin.

Unlike my husband, it's the one and only mark on my skin.

"Princess?" he calls, breaking me out of my thoughts.

"Huh?" I look up at him.

"What do you think?"

My breath catches in my throat as I read the word across his left pec – right across his heart.

Nina.

It's just like mine, but in black ink.

Now our baby will not only be remembered in my mind, but on both of our bodies too – the two bodies that created her life.

"It's perfect," I whisper.

He turns to look at it in the mirror. He runs his finger underneath the reddened patch of skin where his brand new tribute sits.

I watch his expression the entire time that it takes me to reach him.

He looks happy and sad at the same time.

It's a feeling I know well.

I wrap my arms around him from behind and press the side of my face against his back.

"I love you," I murmur.

He turns, and I let him go until he's facing me before wrapping my arms around him again.

"One day, if we have more kids, their names will go right here with their sister's."

I nod but don't say anything. The only thing I want more than for us to have another baby, is him.

I only just got him back and I know I need to enjoy this while it's just the two of us.

We're both young. We've got plenty of time for the rest of it.

I lean in and place a single kiss to his chest and our daughter's name.

"I love you, princess," he whispers.

CHAPTER TWENTY-FIVE

Andy
Two months later

I swing the door open and toss my keys onto the table. "I might have done something stupid, princess," I call out. "Something *really* fucking stupid."

She appears in the doorway and I have to catch my breath. I'd never fucking admit that to anyone – not even her, but I do, every single night when I come home.

I'm so grateful to be here with her, getting a second chance I definitely don't deserve and those feelings slam me hard in the chest each time she walks into a room.

"Hello to you too." She smirks at me.

"No time for formalities, princess, this is important."

"My day was good, thanks, how was yours?" she continues with her little game.

"Jesus Christ, stop fucking around will you?"

She doesn't move an inch, just stands there looking at me with one of her brows arched – waiting for me to give into her ridiculous request, and like the sucker I am, I do exactly as she wants.

"*Fine*, god dammit, woman, how was your day?"

"Mmm... It was alright." She shrugs. "Nothing special."

"Seriously?" I demand. "All the theatrics for *that*?"

She bites back a laugh. "Tell me what stupid shit you've done this time," she prompts.

"You might be pissed," I warn.

"Did it get you arrested?"

I shake my head and smirk at her. "Not this time."

"Then I'll survive."

"I went by our old place."

Her eyes light up. "Oh yeah, how's it look?"

"Good, princess, it looks like home."

She looks at me with a gooey expression on her face, the same way she does when I say something she considers sweet.

"I bought it back," I blurt out.

"You did *what*?"

"I made them an offer and they accepted." I wince.

It really seemed like a good idea at the time – now, not so much.

Buying a house is really something you should ask your wife about first.

Her jaw drops. "You bought our old house?"

"Told you I did something stupid." I shrug.

She's quiet for a pause before a smile spreads across her face. "That was a risk move, Andy... but it's not stupid, it's perfect."

"Yeah?" I ask hopefully.

"Mmm hmm." She nods as she approaches me.

"Well thank fuck for that." I run my hand through my hair in relief.

"*Our* house," she breathes.

"They painted one of the rooms pink, princess, so we're going to have to fucking take care of that shit, but it's *ours*. It's still our home."

She slides her hands around my neck and laughs.

"I can't believe you did that."

"We were happy there, Dylan. That place is filled with us," I reply as I wrap my arms around her body.

She nods her head in agreement. "I would have been happy with you anywhere, but thank you. This is the best of the stupid things you've done so far."

"I'm learning." I wink at her.

"Slowly," she jokes.

"I learned how to wear shirts."

She pouts. "I'm not sure that's a good thing after all."

"You're right, princess, clothes are a *bad* idea."

I reach down with both hands and take hold of the front of her dress.

It's one that domes down the front and when I give it a tug, the whole thing pops open to me.

I look at her body like I've been starved of it.

"*Andy*," she scolds me half-heartedly. "Jeff and Sarah are going to be here in half an hour."

Her mouth might be saying no, but her eyes are saying hell fucking yes.

"We'll be done in twenty."

"You're *never* done in twenty." She laughs as I slide the dress off her shoulder and watch it fall to the floor.

She's not wrong. I'm full of shit. I like to take my time with her these days – savour every second.

"They'll be fine waiting for us," I murmur as I kiss her neck.

"They'll *kill* each other," she argues as she tilts her head back to give me better access. "We're lucky they even agreed to be in the same room."

Her hands have found their way up my t-shirt now, her long nails scratching lightly at my skin.

"Then we'll have dinner with the last one standing." I chuckle.

I reach around and hoist her against me by her perfect ass.

She wraps her legs around my waist and grips onto my neck.

Her lips meet mine and she tugs my bottom lip into her mouth and sucks.

I groan.

"We *can't*," she insists as I head for the bedroom, her in my arms.

"You make a compelling argument, princess, but we already *are*."

"You're going to have to be quick, Drew."

"Don't rush me, woman." I grin at her as I lay her down on the bed.

We both know I'll leave our best friends – two people that hate each other more than anything, waiting for this.

Fuck, I'd keep the Queen waiting for this.

No one and nothing else matters as I strip the underwear off the woman I love.

The place could be burning around me, and I'd still be tugging the t-shirt I knew she'd learn to hate over my head and off.

There's nothing light about her scratches now – those are going to leave a mark.

Every moan of my name only reminds me of how fucking lucky I am to be here.

I want it all with this woman.

I want to fill her up with love and life and babies.

I want a baby.

I want a family and I want it now.

That's the only realisation I need.

"I'm not wearing one," I announce as I pull my hand back from the box of condoms I've just reached for.

She looks at me with a puzzled expression, before a hopeful look crosses her face.

"You're not?" she whispers.

"Nope," I reply. "I'm not; fuck it, you with me, princess?"

She nods quickly, eagerly, like maybe this is something she's wanted for a while now but has been too afraid to ask for.

"I'm gonna put a baby in your belly and then we're gonna have our friends over for an awkward-as-fuck dinner, yeah?"

She giggles. "I'm not sure it works quite that fast."

"Don't insult my sperm," I growl as I push inside her.

Her laughter cuts off abruptly and is replaced with a long moan.

I've made love to this woman – because that's what this is between us – hundreds of times in the past few months alone, but this time feels different.

We're connected on another level now as I push deep inside her. This time is different.

We've moved on from our past, and this moment signifies us moving into a new future. Together.

EPILOGUE

Andy

"Excuse me, sir?"

I turn and see a middle-aged woman, followed by a guy clutching a huge camera, calling out to me from a few metres away.

"Me?" I question her in confusion.

I don't get random women stopping me in the street – a few stares, much to Dylan's distaste, but not being pulled out of a crowd like this.

She nods and speeds up her pace to catch up with us – the man hot on her heels like a shadow.

I look down at Dylan. "You know her, princess?"

"Nope." She shrugs and snuggles a little closer into my side, one hand resting on her pregnant belly as she watches curiously.

"I'm so sorry to interrupt your afternoon," the woman, who is in front of us now says as she looks me up and down. "And this is going to sound a little strange... But can I ask you what you do for a living?"

She's right, it sounds *really* fucking strange.

I frown at her. "Uhh... I'm a mechanic."

"And an ex-con," Dylan mutters under her breath, a shit-eating grin on her face as she looks up at me innocently.

I nudge her gently in the ribs. "Shhh."

"I was exonerated," I explain to the random woman and her side kick.

"*The bad-boy mechanic.*" She smiles to herself. She turns to the guy and winks. "*Perfect.*"

"What's that?" I question with a nervous chuckle.

"Never mind." She shakes her head, her eyes bright and excited. "I've got a question for you..."

She looks at me expectantly, waiting for my name.

"Andy."

"*Andy,*" she repeats with a smile. "How would you feel about being my Mr. January?"

OTHER TITLES

Love like Yours Series
Rushed – Book 1
Pierced – Book 2
Hunted – Book 3
Chased – Book 4

Rock Games Novels
Paper, Scissors, Rock: Vol. 1
Hide and Seek: Vol. 2

My Heart Duet
My Heart Needs
My Heart Wants

Calendar Boys Novels
Mr. January

ACKNOWLEDGEMENTS

The song that inspired this book – Back To You – Selena Gomez. I heard this song and this whole story came to life.

As always I'd like to thank the people around me that support me, my ideas and the work that I do – you all have no idea how grateful I am for your support.

Thanks to the team at Spell Bound Editing, I appreciate your work so much.

To everybody who read this book, thank you, thank you, thank you, I can't express how grateful I am that you take a chance and pick up a book with my name on it.

Thanks for reading and I hope that you continue on through the series to meet the other men!

ABOUT THE AUTHOR

NICOLE S. GOODIN is a romance author and mother of two from Taranaki in the North Island of New Zealand.

In mid-2015, she started to write about a group of characters who wouldn't get out of her head. Her first book, Rushed, was published in mid-2016.

Nicole enjoys long walks on the beach, pillow fights and braiding her friends' hair. She dislikes clichés, talking about herself in the third person, and people who don't understand her sense of humour.

Please feel free to contact her either via her website, email, Instagram, Twitter or on her Facebook page, she would love to hear your feedback. If you're feeling really game, you can even sign up for her newsletter.

Visit www.nicolegoodinauthor.com for more information.

UPCOMING TITLES

Calendar Boys Novels

Mr. February
Mr. March
Mr. April
Mr. May
Mr. June
Mr. July
Mr. August
Mr. September
Mr. October
Mr. November
Mr. December